VENGEANCE CUTS LOOSE

Other books by Joani Ascher:

Vengeance Tastes Sweet
Vengeance Beyond Reason

VENGEANCE CUTS LOOSE

•

Joani Ascher

AVALON BOOKS
NEW YORK

Library of Congress Catalog Card Number: 2003097361
ISBN 0-8034-9649-4

Published by Thomas Bouregy & Co., Inc.
160 Madison Avenue, New York, NY 10016

PRINTED IN THE UNITED STATES OF AMERICA
ON ACID-FREE PAPER
BY HADDON CRAFTSMEN, BLOOMSBURG, PENNSYLVANIA

To my late parents, Arnold and Fanny Wolf, and to my in-laws, Bert and Adeline Ascher, for all their loving encouragement, and to my husband, David, for that and more.

ACKNOWLEDGMENTS

My most grateful thanks to Jane Degnan, Deborah Nolan, and Kim Zito, all excellent writers and wonderful writing partners. To all the "deserving" hairdressers who were the inspiration for this book, thanks. Finally, I would like to thank my family for their patience and editorial assistance, and my editor, Erin Cartwright, for all her perspicacious suggestions.

Chapter One

As she gazed in the mirror, images of herself reflected all around her, haunting her from every angle, mercilessly mocking the way she looked. There was no place to turn, no escape from the glaring truth.

Wally Morris shook her head and laughed. What could she have been thinking? The denim culottes and red plaid blouse that had looked so jaunty on the lanky mannequin in the store made her five-foot frame look choppy. Worse, while she tried assiduously to watch her weight, the outfit emphasized the unflattering spread that was accumulating around her hips.

Adding insult to injury, she'd spent her entire morning gluing Mother's Day gifts and dispensing snacks to the four and five-year-olds in her class and then had no time to put herself back together before picking up her mother-in-law, Tillie, for her hair appointment. Now, leaning against one of the pink interior walls of the Resplendence Salon & Spa, one of the swankiest beauty salons in Northern New Jersey, her image reflected back at her from at least ten mirrors. She sighed and comforted herself with a complimentary muffin as she waited for Tillie's seven-stage process to be completed.

Wally was only there because Tillie had a broken right leg and couldn't drive. Tillie had insisted on keeping her hair appointment today, because if she didn't get her perm right away, a little over four weeks before her granddaughter's wedding, her hair would not be perfect on that very important day.

As mother of Debbie, the bride-to-be, Wally had her own cause for high anxiety. The gray roots asserting themselves into her Sable Mist hair made her appreciate that she had an appointment of her own to keep. Her appointment was tomorrow, at a different salon, where special attention would be given to the troublesome left side of her chin length hair which flipped up instead of under.

The slight evidence of her roots seemed magnified under the lights, as she surveyed all the smiling women around her being transformed by the various hairdressers, manicurists and facial artists. Shifting her gaze from her own reflection, she surveyed the activity.

Her eye was caught by the young man who was sweeping clumps of hair from the floor. He pushed the broom into a corner and started to remove the lipstick stained coffee cups that were left all around. The busboy, or whatever a person who did this young man's job was called, wore head phones and his body jerked to a rap beat instead of swaying to normal music. Wally tried not to stare at the safety pin in his eyebrow and glanced away, only to find herself looking at the ear of one of the hairdressers. There must have been twenty silver hoops working their way up and around the top of her ear. A slender chain linked her ear to a stud in her nose.

If Wally wasn't so busy, she wouldn't have minded going to the salon with Tillie. It seemed that there were a million things to take care of this afternoon, such as calling the florist, the photographer, the caterer, and the band in order to to fill them in on the latest changes that Debbie had decided to make.

The outer door opened, interrupting Wally's mental checklist, and a woman wearing a business suit, anklets and sneakers came in. Crystal, the receptionist, whose hair was a light, obviously artificial shade of cherry, and whose make-up was chalk white with black lipstick that matched her nails and gave her lips a pucker shape, smiled broadly at her. It transformed her frightening countenance completely—underneath all that makeup she was quite pretty. "Janis," she said, using her first name as all the other employees did on almost all of the customers, "back so soon?"

Janis frowned uncertainly. "I, uh . . ." She started to turn back toward the door.

"Did you, like, forget something?" Crystal prompted. "Your coat?"

That question struck Wally as odd, since it was a gorgeous spring day outside, and at least seventy degrees. It seemed unlikely that Janis had forgotten a coat.

Having nothing better to do, since Tillie's hair was still being rolled onto the perm rods, Wally took a closer look at the woman standing there. She thought she detected an English accent. Janis, who looked like she was in her early forties, shook her head at Crystal's inquiry. "My hair . . ."

The chalk-faced woman studied Janis's brown hair. "It looks very nice."

"No."

"No?"

"It isn't what I wanted," said Janis, confirming Wally's suspicions about her accent. "I told him, several times and very specifically, but he didn't listen. Now look." She turned to show the whole coif.

Wally looked too, although she couldn't say exactly what was wrong. The hair was really short in front, with tiny, undersized bangs commonly found on five-year-olds. But what struck Wally as odd was how asymmetrical the style was, very daring, some would say striking, although the term 'jarring' was more apt.

"Logan, could you come here please?" Crystal said quietly into the phone. She hung up and smiled again at Janis. "Logan will be right with you. He's the owner and he'll fix, uh . . . It'll be okay."

Janis nodded. There were tears in her eyes. "I told him not to cut my bangs so short, but he did. I don't understand that. And I don't understand why he left one side long and made the other side so short. He said he did it because I have an uneven chin, but so what? He said he left the back like this to offset my . . ." Here she gestured with her hand, as if there was some huge thing on her nose, which was not, in Wally's opinion, unusually large. It was, however, natural, not like some of the tiny noses that came out of some doctors' offices. "What does he think I was here for, plastic surgery? I only wanted a hair cut!"

Crystal smiled, somewhat unconvincingly. "Can I, like, get you a cup of coffee?"

Janis stopped gesturing and wiping her eyes long enough to shake her head. "I only wanted a trim." She turned to Wally as if looking for a sympathetic ear. "I can't understand this place. First I have to get used to saying the name of the town as *Gross Venor*, which is totally wrong, and now this! I have a good mind to tell my husband that we are moving back to London."

Wally knew that many people thought that the name of the town was mispronounced. But there were several towns like that in the area. After all, Bogota, New Jersey, was pronounced *buh-Goat-a*. But that didn't explain the hair cut. She smiled at Janis and shrugged.

Logan arrived at the reception desk and assessed the situation. His dapper appearance was enhanced by the white physician's jacket he wore open, emphasizing the starched collar of his shirt and the many heavy gold chains draped across his chest. The dark hairs underneath looked positively unruly in comparison to the sprayed and carefully styled salt-and-pepper hair of his head.

He assumed a position of superiority. "May I help you?"

"My hair!" Janis shouted. "Look what he did to my hair!"

"Who cut your hair?" said Logan, in a half whisper, as if encouraging Janis to lower her voice.

Janis looked around and spotted the offender. She gestured at him with her hand, while he remained, stiff backed, facing away from her. "Garth. I thought it was okay when I left, until I saw it in the mirror of my car when I was going back to work. I mean, he seemed to say it was good, and I didn't really look because he was making such a fuss about how terrific it was, but look at it!"

"We'll fix it right up," said Logan, as he glared across the room at Garth. Following his gaze, Wally saw a handsome thirty-something man, with long bleached hair on top of his head and brown close-shaved hair underneath. It occurred to Wally that with his lean muscular physique and flat stomach, evident under his tight, black tee shirt, he could be on the cover of one of those Harlequin novels that Tillie loved. Except Harlequin men didn't usually sneer.

As Logan guided Janis past Garth and all the other operator stations to the back of the salon, he passed an elderly woman with a cane and nearly pink hair. She did not pause to let the two people pass. Instead, they had to press themselves against the corridor wall to let her get by. Janis avoided looking at Garth as they stood facing his station, but he, on the other hand, made a face at her. Wally wondered if his boss saw that.

A short time later, a door closed behind Wally and she realized that Logan and his dissatisfied customer must have gone around the back of the salon and along the other corridor to a cubicle directly on the other side of the wall that she was leaning on. She supposed that made sense. The hall, which went all the way to the back of the store, near the outer rear entrance, followed around in a U-shape past the spa rooms and back toward the reception area. The cublicle could have been reached more easily by going around the front of the salon, but Wally presumed that Logan hadn't wanted to walk teary-eyed Janis past the people sitting in the lounge waiting area. One woman, who had been filling out one of the lengthy applications that new clients were asked to submit, had already picked up her purse and left. If Janis had gone the other way, there was no telling how many more defectors there might have been.

The noise level in the salon rose as the people beside her realized the confrontation was over. Now, as they went back to their own conversations, Wally heard snippets of what they said.

"Did I tell you I got it done?" someone said.

"No way."

The two voices came from the chair opposite from where Tillie sat. The hairdresser, looking straggly and disheveled, was talking to a prematurely gray woman whose hair he was cutting.

"Yes, I said I would and I did it. I got the tummy tuck. Do you want to see?"

The woman nodded eagerly. The hairdresser turned the chair she was sitting in and faced her. "You are not going to believe this, and there is no scar." He lift his tee shirt, revealing his midriff. "Look, it's all gone."

The man's stomach was right at the female customer's eye level and she had a close look.

"Wow, that's amazing."

"It's still a little swollen," he said, pulling his tee shirt down. "And it hurt like heck." He gestured his head in Garth's direction. "He thinks I'm crazy. Like it's any of his business."

The woman made sympathetic noises. After a few more minutes, while the hairdresser cut the front of the customer's hair, she spoke again. "What happened with that guy?"

"He said he would move in."

"No way."

"He needed a place and I offered. He said yes."

"No way."

Standing behind her, the man studied her face in the mirror as he continued to trim her hair. "I got everything all ready, and then he called and said he was taking a place with someone else."

"Oh, I'm so sorry."

"Yeah. It was too bad. I was gonna feel him out, see if he was, like, interested. But I guess not."

"Wally?" Tillie called. "I need help." Tillie's head was swathed in cotton and plastic, but her cheery face showed that she knew that her daughter-in-law had been eavesdropping.

Wally jumped, embarrassed. "Okay. Let's get you turned."

Tillie's hairdresser, a lovely woman named Eunice who wore full false eyelashes and lots of eye shadow, pressed the release to lower Tillie's chair. Wally helped her stand up, and handed her the crutches that were leaning against the wall. "Just take her over to that chair," said Eunice, pointing at a chair underneath a contraption which resembled nothing short of a medieval instrument of torture. "That will help your perm along," she explained, after seeing the look of skepticism on Tillie's face. "It's new."

Wally caught a whiff of the solution used to transform Tillie's hair from straight to curly. It smelled like perfumed rotten eggs, not significantly different from the solutions that Wally's late mother Judith had used for years. That odor, mingled with all the other smells in the salon, formed a pungent mix as Wally helped Tillie over to the chair.

Ordinarily, Tillie was perfectly capable of taking care of herself, getting to the hairdresser in her own car, which, although she was eighty-three, she drove quite well. That was impossible now, since the incident involving an overflowing washing machine, three senior citizens, and a flight of stairs. Luckily it was a clean break, and with any luck, Tillie would have the cast off her leg the week before Debbie's wedding.

The long awaited event—when Debbie Morris, by that date *Esquire*, would marry Elliot Levine, also Esquire—would be perfect, Wally thought. Everything was nearly set. The dresses were almost ready, including the dresses that the matron of honor, Debbie's sister Rachel, and the flower girl, Rachel's daughter, would wear. Elliot's parents were due up from Florida in another week, and the final arrangements would be made then. They were wonderful people, and Wally was sure that Debbie would never have problems with her in-laws.

Wally counted herself among those lucky people who didn't have those problems. Her father-in-law had been a true gentleman, and Tillie was warm and loving. Taking care of her was a privilege, even though there were a million other things to be done. Tillie had never turned Wally down when she needed help, and Wally wouldn't turn her down now.

A ding of the timer indicated that Tillie, or at least her hair, was fully cooked. Eunice came over and together she and Wally got Tillie over to the sink to have her hair rinsed. After a new solution was put on to neutralize the first one, and Tillie was back under the dryer, Wally allowed her attention to wander again.

The salon had become more crowded, with people in almost

every chair. Customers were having facials, pedicures, and manicures as well as work done on their hair. One woman had evidently sent her hair alone, because a stylist was working hard on a wig. The busboy was going from station to station, replacing used towels with clean ones. An elderly woman asked him to get her a bagel when he had a chance. She called him Dakota.

Wally felt she was in the way and went to stand against the wall again. From that spot it wasn't hard to listen in to another conversation. This one was between another woman Wally knew and her hairdresser. Wally had once gone to that hairdresser, a tall blond with big brown eyes, and knew that she went by the name of Marigold.

"She's just got out of the hospital last week," said Marigold. "I'm surprised she's back."

"She's been through this before," said the black-caped woman whose hair was being painted with a dark dye.

"This time I think it was because of him," said Marigold.

"You mean Garth? I thought they broke up long ago."

"You're right, Irene, they did, but they were trying the let's-be-friends thing. He said he was kidding when he told her she was fat. But let me ask you this: how many brains does it take to know that you don't tell someone who has been fighting bulimia that she's fat? Some friend."

Wally felt a thud on the wall behind her and shifted uncomfortably. She was getting tired of standing there, but there were no available chairs to sit in, even under a dryer. She looked at her watch, and realized she still had a long time to go. Maybe she could get away for a few minutes, if Tillie was seated somewhere and didn't need her for a while.

There was another thud, which left her wondering what was going on in that consultation room, but she decided it was better not to think about it. Janis had come out some time before, looking marginally better but with a big smile on her face. Maybe some other haircut disaster was being rectified behind closed doors. "I wonder who is being rescued this time," Wally said.

"What did you say, dear?" asked Tillie.

"I just wondered who was in the consultation room making all that noise."

"I didn't hear anything," said Tillie, who often didn't, due to failing hearing, "did you, Eunice?"

Tillie's hairdresser shrugged. "I don't hear much of anything. I try to mind my own business."

Wally had a momentary sense of rebuke, just as the timer went off again, indicating that it was time for Tillie's hair to be rinsed. As they pulled out the rods, Wally decided to take a little walk as soon as she could. Tillie's silvery hair would need to be set, and dried, a process which would take over an hour.

Several people passed them as she slowly led Tillie back to Eunice's chair. Many people were waiting in the lounge area, drinking their coffee, and other people walked purposefully all over the place. Deliveries arrived, some having to be signed for, and the phone never stopped ringing. Poor Crystal was pulled in six different directions, but, to her credit, she smiled through most of it.

The Morrises had to wait for the changing room so that Tillie could change her blue getting-a-perm smock for a pink having-a-set one. Her silvery hair was a lovely color, so she never needed a black getting-hair-color smock.

By the time they got back to the chair, Tillie was positively tired. "I haven't walked much since I broke my leg," she said. "Everyone has been doing all the walking for me."

"You rest while you're under the dryer," said Wally. "I'll be back in a little while."

"What?"

Wally repeated what she had said, louder.

"Okay," said Tillie. "I won't go anywhere." She smiled at her own joke.

Wally smiled back, and scooted away. If she hurried, she could get those calls made, or maybe buy something for dinner. She rounded the corner and started on her way to the back entrance of the salon and the parking lot. Suddenly she heard screams.

"Another bad haircut?" she asked Crystal, who was attempting to rush past her. Crystal did not respond, but Wally was convinced she saw a trace of a smile on those blackened lips.

Once Wally got to the center of the commotion, all of her plans to do errands evaporated, cut short by the continued screams of a woman who was staring into the consultation room at the grotesque face of the newly deceased body of Garth Barkley.

Chapter Two

Wally stood in the doorway of Consultation Room A, blocking the way so that no one else could enter. No one seemed inclined to anyway. Most of the women who had come running when Irene screamed stood looking squeamishly at each other and reminding Wally of people rubbernecking while driving past an accident. She looked at her watch, hoping that Dominique Scott, Elliot's partner when he was on the local police force, would be the detective who responded to the frantic call that had been placed by Crystal.

Irene Cummins was someone who Wally knew from her days on the PTA. It became apparent that her trip to the ladies' room had been cut short by her nosy peek past the open door of the consultation room where Garth had sat bleeding to death. The poor woman was sobbing loudly against Marigold's shoulder, oblivious to her hair coloring timer, which dinged five minutes earlier. Marigold's blouse was ruined by the Flameout hair dye, but she comforted her client nevertheless.

The black marble counter tops of the room glowed faintly under special lighting used to soften age lines and make women feel pretty after their pampering. Light spilling in from the open door illuminated the room further, enabling the mirror to reflect the horrible contents centered within. Garth's body slumped on a plastic molded chair. The corpse wore a black plastic cape that was pushed askew, revealing the shiny handles of a pair of scissors sticking out of the center of his chest. Blood stained the front of the shirt and dripped down, pooling in the curves of the chair.

The strong scent of permanent wave solution masked most of the odor of blood and other bodily emissions of Garth, but not all. Despite her previous close encounters with murder investigations, Wally had never seen a murder victim before, and she fought the urge to vomit. Garth's grotesque countenance, plainly visible in the mirror opposite the chair, was awful to see.

Dominique Scott, whose gorgeous brown face and fantastic figure made people wonder why she was a police detective instead of a model, came into the corridor, just after the first police officers and the rescue squad arrived. She pushed past the fifteen women, who all swore they couldn't possibly look at the body but didn't move away, over to where Wally stood at the doorway, next to Logan, the owner of the salon.

"I might have known," said Dominique, as the EMTs packed up their useless, in this case, equipment. She cocked her head to one side, as if to say it did not look like Wally was having beautifying work done. "What are you doing here?"

Wally walked with her to the front of the salon and pointed to Tillie, still under the hair dryer, her large print *Reader's Digest* propped up even though she was snoozing and completely unaware of the commotion. "Waiting."

Dominique nodded. "We have to clear the area so we can get to work," she said, herding all the other onlookers away from the corridor in front of the consultation rooms. "The county guys will be here soon."

There was more than a trace of regret on Dominique's face as she said that. Wally knew how it upset Dominique to be second fiddle on investigations, but that was how it worked in murder cases. And Wally should know, since this was the third murder in a little over three years in Grosvenor, an otherwise law abiding community.

Wally followed all the people, many in various stages of glamorization, some with rollers, some with hair dye, some waving partially painted wet nails, out of the front area of the salon. She went over to stand near Tillie, to keep out of the way as much as possible.

Tillie's eyes were closed as she continued to snooze peacefully under the bubble-hooded dryer. From where she sat, even if she had her eyes open, all she would have been able to see were the backs of people craning to see the police team. Wally wished she could watch the procedures, but, on second thought, realized she was just as happy that she didn't have to see the body and the room again.

A few of the employees were crying in the back of the salon near the door. Wally could see them clearly, and made a mental note of which ones weren't at their stations and which ones carried on. She wasn't checking to see who was a good little trooper, who could keep the shop humming even in the face of adversity; she was looking to see who might have some particular feelings about Garth's murder. Amateur detective, that's what Nate would accuse her of being. On that score, however, he could rest his mind—there simply was no time or reason for Wally to do more than speculate about this case, unlike all the work she did on those other murders. Hopefully none of this would affect her at all, aside from a simple statement she'd probably have to make to the police.

Elliot Levine pushed back his desk chair as far as it could go before it hit the wall. With considerable maneuvering he was able to get his tall, lean frame out from behind the desk. Of all the days to be called to see Marshall, the assistant prosecutor, this was the worst. He had to be at the tuxedo store for his fitting appointment by 5:30 and it was already after 4:00. If Marshall, a highly ambitious man, got started, he could go on for hours. He wouldn't be in line for a promotion or an elected position unless all those under him gave more than 100%. Elliot had been working on an interesting case, going over evidence and researching case law, and even though it was relatively clear cut, he was putting everything he had into it. He didn't see how he could give more, but he knew he'd be asked.

So he was very surprised when instead of being interrogated about the case in Montclair, Marshall told Elliot about a new case, a murder, in his own town. Speaking in soft but serious tones, with an appropriately serious look on his face, Marshall could have been explaining the situation to the evening news reporters. With his carefully tailored suit and perfectly straight tie, he did not look like a man going about his business behind closed doors in his own office. He looked like what he was—thirty-eight-year-old aspiring politician, ever ready to sweet-talk the public.

"The bottom line," Marshall told Elliot, "is that I don't care what you're working on. I want you to drop it and get right on this case." He stopped when someone knocked on the door.

When the door opened, Elliot found himself looking at the lean, wiry body and hyper tense face of Inspector Davis of the Essex County Sheriff's Department. Although they had shared cases since Elliot went to the prosecutor's office, Elliot felt residual antagonism emanating from Davis for the way he'd handled the investigation of the murder in Grosvenor the year before. Elliot suspected that Davis was still smarting from having the local police detectives solve two widely publicized cases that the county couldn't crack.

"Have you told him?" Davis asked, his tone implying that the antagonism between them had not diminished.

Marshall smiled, revealing perfectly aligned teeth. "Just now."

Davis went to stand beside the assistant prosecutor in what Elliot took as a show of force.

"For a change," Davis growled, "we, and I mean the county, are going to solve a murder case in Grosvenor, your little town of murders." He chuckled, indicating that maybe somewhere deep in his heart, he had a sense of humor. "Even if we have to use the former detective who solved those other cases."

Elliot remained silent, afraid of saying something that would bring out Marshall's true sadistic nature, or worse, Davis's ire. It didn't help, because just as Elliot reached the door, Davis added, "You're one of ours now, don't forget it. You work for the county, not this little two bit town bureaucracy." He turned to Marshall and winked. "I'm on my way. We're gonna nail this one."

Within a half hour from the time of the 911 call, Crystal noticed that the town of Grosvenor had begun to fill up with news trucks from all the local television stations as well as representatives of the radio and print media. She found it exciting having famous television people standing right outside the window.

B. J. Waters stepped out of a news van parked illegally in the center of town and a few seconds later she transmitted the first teaser for the evening news.

The television camera panned the street near the salon before focusing on B. J., who wore a light summer suit in a shade of peach. People stopped nearby, some not quite out of camera range, and watched as the reporter spoke into the camera, reading from her notes.

"Turn it up," said Armond, one of the older male hairdressers. The person nearest the small television in the waiting area pushed the volume button.

"This is B. J. Waters, and I am in the town of Grosvenor, New Jersey, where a murder has recently occurred. This tiny Essex County town has been the site of two previous murders in as many years, and trouble has returned today. Watch the five o'clock news for a live report on the death of a popular young man."

Crystal watched from inside the salon as the reporter motioned to the cameraman to stop taping, and saw B. J. turn to the crowd of spectators. The small TV had returned to normal programming and someone turned down the sound. Two women who were watching it went to look out the window.

Less than five minutes later, another reporter with another camera crew began broadcasting from outside the salon, while Crystal and a small group of people inside watched. Crystal easily figured out which station to tune to because the channel number on the side of the van was enormous. While the murder made Crystal feel awful, her skin prickled with the thought of being on the news, even if she couldn't be seen. She dialed her mother's phone number.

By the time Wally got Tillie back to her apartment building, it seemed that all her neighbors had heard the news about Garth. Since Tillie was the first resident who had been on the scene when the murder happened, she became the center of attention, even though she had slept through almost the entire commotion. Tillie, however, managed to sound knowledgeable since while Eunice combed out Tillie's hair, she reviewed everything that happened, with embellishment from Wally.

Dominique had promised she would question Wally as soon as possible, but there were many people to question, so many who were potential witnesses. All of them had been asked to stay in the salon until they could complete a questionnaire prepared by Dominique and her new partner, Ryan Devlin. Several people had complained about the questionnaire, including a former English teacher who found it had grammatical and spelling errors. Wally wished they would give the detectives a break.

The body had finally been removed and the questionnaires collected. Dominique and the rest of the local police department had been pushed aside by Inspector Davis from the county sheriff's office, but he seemed to be much more civil than in previous cases. He said something to Dominique and she laughed, before turning and giving Wally a wink. Everyone was allowed to go about their business and Wally took Tillie home.

"Did you see who did it, Tillie?" asked a gray-haired lady. Actually, thought Wally, they were nearly all gray-haired, or artificially pale blond.

Tillie knit her brow. "No. But I saw Garth just before he died."

Wally wondered how true that could be, since the police weren't entirely sure how long he had been dead. Death might not have come as soon as he was stabbed, and no one had admitted, at least not yet, what time they last saw Garth, or last went into Consultation Room A.

Another lady, whose name was Emma if Wally remembered correctly, said, "Tillie, you should go in and sit down. You shouldn't stand on that leg."

All the other women agreed and they helped Tillie inside. "Come along," said Tillie.

"I should be getting home," Wally replied. "Nate will want to talk to me." She didn't add that Nate would probably want to talk her out of involving herself in another murder investigation. But he had no need to worry. As much as she wanted to solve the puzzle, she didn't feel a compelling interest in this case.

Chapter Three

Rita Barkley put down the phone in shock. The slimeball was dead. She couldn't think of anything in the world that made her more unhappy. She had missed her opportunity to kill him herself, something she had daydreamed about over the course of years. Every stair step exercise she took in her aerobics class went to the same beat—up, down, back, forward, back—*get Garth, make him pay*.

Of all the rip-offs that had occurred to her in the past, this was the biggest one ever. Not only had she been subjected to four years of torture as his wife, she had been the lucky recipient of all of his debts, including a rather hefty one to the IRS. They did not care that a divorce decree had been granted since she had stupidly signed her name to their joint tax returns. In addition, she had lost her home, courtesy of Garth's fraudulent attempt to collect on a fire insurance policy, as well as every one of the friends she had before she married the snake.

But now she had the chance to smile at his funeral. That would be one event she would not miss. She began to imagine a jazzercise routine danced on his grave.

Through her tears, Sally Barkley could barely find the cradle to hang up the phone. She located it blindly, then put her head down over it and sobbed, railing against her fate. It couldn't be true, there was no way Garth could be dead. He was so virile, so strong. She could have said exactly how strong, since she'd felt his strength whenever he packed it into a punch aimed at her.

It wasn't his fault, she knew. It was his ex-wife Rita's, who drove him to distraction and made him so short-tempered. Sally tried so hard to be the best wife and mother she could but sometimes she didn't quite make it and he had to punish her. It really was no one's business but her own, yet her parents had interfered and forced her to leave Garth. She knew they meant well, and as the only child of well-off parents she had never wanted for anything, both before and after her failed marriage. Well maybe one thing—Garth. Sally had always planned for her and Madeline to go back to him, never to get a divorce. She was shocked when he divorced her while she was gone, in order to marry that other woman. Almost as much of a shock as hearing that he was dead. Now she'd never get him back. He could never be her husband again, or the terrific father he was to their little girl, when he was able to clear his busy schedule to see her for an afternoon. Too bad that was only every six months or so.

The worst part was, how would she tell Madeline that her beloved Daddy was dead?

Tess Barkley, the third Mrs. Garth Barkley, took the phone off the hook and put it into the junk drawer. She had already fielded calls from her five sisters and her mother, two aunts and her eighty-seven-year-old grandmother. The last thing she wanted was to hear from anyone else about what they considered to be great news.

Not that the news wasn't great. It was such a relief, in a way, to learn that Garth would no longer be a part of her life, or Lisa's. Not only wouldn't she have to put up with his temper tantrums about whom she was dating, she wouldn't have to share Lisa with him four times a month. He could also no longer finagle his way into those little loans he always needed and never repaid. Tess barely had enough money for her rent most months, since she was stretched so thin, thanks to Garth. He was so far behind on child support that Lisa couldn't take the ballet lessons she so badly wanted.

It occurred to her that someone must have been mighty incensed by him, but that did not surprise her. There must have been at least twenty people in the last few years alone who were irate enough to kill him. That didn't even include people he had taken advantage of or hurt, whose stories he had repeated gleefully over and over, as if warning her not to cross him.

She should have listened before she got involved with him. But he was so handsome and so sophisticated that she ignored the warnings of her family and allowed herself to fall in love with him. During the three years that she stayed with him after Lisa was born, he abused, bullied, and essentially tortured her. Since then it hadn't been much better as they were still tied closely by their little girl.

Now Tess was free. It seemed like a celebration was in order. But not with her family. So, still leaving the phone off the hook, she picked up the keys to her battered, barely running car. She had half an hour before she had to pick up Lisa from her play date, time to at least drive past the place where he was killed and gloat, big time.

But as she put her key into her car door lock, another thought occurred to her, a thought which let every single molecule of air out of her happiness balloon. Someone had done her and everyone else in town a favor, and someone would have to pay.

Debbie's voice on the phone was demanding. "How could you?"

Judging from her tone, Wally pictured her blond daughter, angry and poised to fight.

"I didn't mean to," Wally said sincerely, while wracking her brain to try to figure out what mistake she had made. As far as she knew, she was up to date, or nearly, with all the caterers, florists, photographers and musicians. What she had done wrong to merit Debbie's tone escaped her.

"You just can't help yourself, can you?"

The accusation sounded as if she had just been caught eating a pint of Ben and Jerry's ice cream single-handedly, which, based on the grumbling in her stomach, hadn't happened. "Help myself what?"

"You just can't stay away from trouble or keep out of other people's business."

A shred of illumination hit Wally. "You mean the murder. It wasn't my fault that I got involved. I'm really not, you know, involved. Neither is your grandmother. Don't worry, it won't affect you, or your wedding. I promise." Nate had made the same kind of insinuation when Wally finally returned home from Tillie's. He'd also implied that not only was she incapable of staying out of trouble, she had now dragged his eighty-three-year-old temporarily disabled mother into it.

Wally had mustered a supreme effort not to argue with her husband, who was, in her opinion, being more than a little unreasonable. Although she felt terrible for the murdered man and everyone else involved, she had no intention of getting enmeshed herself. But she kept that to herself, refusing to consider putting the obvious into words.

Now another person didn't believe that this really wouldn't affect their lives.

"It isn't only you!" Debbie said. "You've gotten Elliot involved too!"

Ice water streamed through Wally's veins, sending shivers up and down her spine even though it had to be at least seventy-five degrees in the kitchen. "You can't be serious! How?"

"Because the assistant prosecutor wants his friends over in the Sheriff's office to stop being incompetent. They don't like it when the DA's office looks inept for preparing cases against innocent people. Elliot is supposed to help pinpoint the real killer. They want him completely involved in the investigation—as a detective."

Wally was having a hard time trying to understand just exactly how this was her fault, but she knew better than to challenge Debbie on that.

"I'm sorry."

Fervently hoping that the technique for placating her spouse would work on her daughter, she waited for a response.

"I wasn't thinking. I should have made sure I was elsewhere." That last bit was delivered with a trace of sarcasm that Wally hoped would not be detectable to Debbie over the phone.

"Well, you had to be with Nana," said Debbie, thoughtfully. "She can't get around by herself."

"Maybe I should have sent your father," Wally suggested.

"He would have hated that."

Wally laughed almost giddily, relieved that the tension was decreasing. "I think you're right."

"And he really couldn't have prevented the murder," said Debbie, almost to herself. "Could he?"

The thought sobered Wally. "I know I couldn't. You know I wish it hadn't happened, especially now that it has Elliot involved."

"He's kind of happy," Debbie admitted. "Now that he's a prosecutor, he's been missing the investigative police work."

Wally heard the doorbell ring. "Walk with me," she said to Debbie, as the family's black Labrador retriever, Sammy, ran to the front door. "I'm on my way to answer the door." Since she was on the portable phone, she was able to continue her conversation as she walked toward the living room.

"Ooh," said Debbie. "Maybe it's the UPS man with more presents for me."

"The UPS man is a woman," Wally reminded her. "You've seen Niki, haven't you?"

"I think so. She's about my age, a little taller, with dark hair?"

Wally chuckled at her barely five-foot tall daughter's big aspirations. "Actually, she's over thirty, and way taller." Wally pushed the dog aside and pulled open the door.

She had spotted the UPS truck through the front windows, and smiled in anticipation. If this wasn't another present for Debbie, it might be something for Nate, an avid catalogue shopper.

To her surprise, the brown-clad delivery person was not Niki Stetson. The man held out an electronic clip board, waited for Wally's signature, and handed over a large box addressed to Debbie with a Tiffany's return address.

"Thanks," she said, closing the door. "Do you want me to open this box from Tiffany's?" she said casually into the phone.

Debbie squealed. "Stop. Don't touch it. I'll be home tonight. Elliot and I will be there right after his tux appointment." After a short pause, but before Wally could say goodbye, Debbie added a dig: "If he can get off."

Chastised again, Wally fervently wished that she could talk to someone who would completely believe her when she said that she wanted nothing to do with the latest trouble in Grosvenor, but her friend Louise Fisch was out of town on a trip. That she could fly off to Hawaii at such a critical time in Wally's life was certainly annoying. How could she wait four and a half weeks for her friend's return?

In the meantime, she had several things to do. Debbie had decided that she wanted more color in the flowers of her chuppah, the traditional wedding canopy under which the bride and groom stand while they are married. Several calls to the florist had gone unreturned so Wally sat down to dial again.

"Mrs. Morris," said the florist, after Wally had insisted that she would wait until the woman could speak to her. "Your daughter specifically said that she wanted all white flowers, calla lilies, lilies of the valley, baby's breath and white roses."

"I know. But now she wants it to match her bridesmaids' bouquets. She'd like pinks, lavenders, purples, and if you have anything that goes, some blues."

"I suppose I can get them, there's still time to change the order, but I won't be able to do it again. Is she absolutely sure?"

Wally wondered but she answered anyway, as convincingly as she could. "Yes."

"You don't sound so sure."

"I'm just wondering how it will look," Wally confessed. "I

guess I'm used to the all-white look. That's what Rachel, my other daughter, had."

"I remember. It was lovely. But that wedding was in winter, and this one is in June. This will be absolutely gorgeous, I guarantee it."

That assurance notwithstanding, Wally still had a few questions for the florist. When she was done, she felt slightly better, until the phone rang.

"Mrs. Morris?"

The warm voice on the other end of the line could only belong to Dominique Scott. As much as Wally enjoyed talking to her, she knew that this would not be a social call. Even though the Morrises had become friendly with Dominique and her husband James, and had even started seeing James professionally when their old dentist retired, this was not a call to chat.

"How is the case going?" asked Wally. "Did you find the murderer yet?"

"I wish. This could be really difficult. We're hoping forensic evidence will help us narrow down the list of suspects."

"There can't have been that many," said Wally.

"But there were. I've gone over the lists everyone left identifying people they saw. Even assuming that someone saw the person who turns out to have killed Garth Barkley, and remembered and wrote the name down, there are scores of people."

"Really?"

"There were so many customers and service people, and the back door opens to the parking lot. Some people were seen just walking through the salon to get to the street, or from the street back through to the lot."

Wally had done that herself several times. It saved walking around the block. "But those people couldn't have stopped to do something like that. How would they have known that Garth would be in that room?"

"It would be easier if we could eliminate them on that basis," Dominique said, "but we can't. Someone could have lured him into the room, saying he or she needed to talk. The receptionist . . ."

"Crystal," Wally said, supplying the name to save Dominique from having to go through her notes.

"Thanks, right. Crystal said that she can't see the back door from her desk, and that there's no way of knowing how long it takes any given person to walk through. We have a list of names of the people seen by the ladies in the waiting area, but that might not be complete if the person walked around the other way."

Wally was beginning to see the problem. "Anyone could have done this, and that person might not have even been seen?"

"Possibly, though I don't really think so. People probably saw the murderer, although that doesn't mean that it registered in their minds or that they wrote that name down. We have to interview everyone and we may have to question people a second time as we develop leads."

"Are you saying that this could take a while?"

"Yes."

Wally opened the oven door to check on dinner. "You've heard?"

"That Elliot has been assigned to this case? Yes." She was quiet for a minute and Wally, who was turning down the temperature on the oven, was momentarily distracted. So she was startled when Dominique suddenly whispered, "It's making my new partner even crazier than usual."

"What do you mean?"

"Ryan is, uh, kind of insecure."

Wally remembered the red-haired detective who had come into the salon with Dominique. He had sharp, pleasant features under his freckles—what Tillie would call good bone structure—red hair and very blue eyes, as well as a good build, but it had occurred to her that he was uncomfortable. She figured that was because he was surrounded by women having things done to themselves that men don't usually see before they are finished. But he'd asked his questions professionally enough and it surprised Wally that Dominique would characterize him as insecure.

"He's still new," said Wally.

"I know. I'm not questioning his ability. I think he'll be very good, but he doesn't seem to be so sure. And now he's doing that thing again."

"What thing?"

"He's asking me every two minutes what Elliot would do. I try never to talk about him, but Ryan seems to think that Elliot is some kind of god. He used to think that way about me, too, but I guess spending so much time with me has straightened him out."

"He'll probably get straight about Elliot too," said Wally. "Not that I don't adore my future son-in-law." Dominique's predictions bothered her. "I just hope this case doesn't interfere with the wedding."

"We won't let it, Mrs. Morris," Dominique assured her. "Not if we can help it."

"Just let me know if I can help," said Wally.

"Do you have any thoughts on the subject?" Dominique asked.

"Well, I . . ." Wally stopped as a realization hit her. "Oh!"

"What?"

"I take that back. I can't help. I don't have the time. I don't want to. Don't let me. If you see me coming, turn the other way."

Dominique laughed. "I hear you, but it isn't that simple. You were there. You wouldn't want to shirk your civic duty, would you?"

"That's a good one. I'll have to use that on Nate the next time he criticizes me about this. And if I guess right, that should be soon. Here he comes."

Nate was coming out of his office in the barn behind the Morris home. Sammy blew through the ill-fitting screen door and scampered around him, racing after a Frisbee that Nate threw periodically, whenever Sammy relinquished the plastic disk long enough.

"I'll let you go then," said Dominique.

Wally had just finished saying goodbye when Nate walked in. He looked so fit and handsome, with his silvery hair, twinkling blue eyes and, since he hadn't met with anyone professionally all day, his form fitting jeans and work shirt. Asking innocently, "Need any help with dinner?" he seemed willing to let go of the earlier discussion they'd had and Wally was just as happy to leave things as they were. She hated it when there was tension between them, but a quick test of the air led her to believe it was clear.

She smiled. "Just as soon as you give me my hug."

Chapter Four

"Topping our news tonight," said the serious-faced 6:00 news anchor, "is another murder in the small town of Grosvenor, New Jersey."

The camera angle changed, and the anchor turned. "Police are questioning dozens of people in the afternoon murder of . . ." he paused, consulting his notes, "Garth Barkley, a prominent businessman, hairstylist and partner at the Resplendence Salon and Spa. No motive has been determined at this time. Many people were present during the incident and all will be questioned. For more on this, we go live to B. J. Waters in Grosvenor. B. J.?"

The picture on the screen changed to a woman wearing a peach suit and standing in front of Resplendence. Wally, watching the television in her kitchen, swallowed hard seeing it like that. It vividly reminded her of what she saw when she was there. But she was unable to turn off the television so she watched B. J. Waters, the reporter she'd seen too often in her town over the past two years, give her report.

"Thanks, John," said B. J. "Well, as you know, Garth Barkley worked here," she gestured behind her toward the storefront, "at Resplendence, a luxury hair salon and spa. But he was more than a mere employee. He was also one of the partners. By all accounts, his services were very much in demand." She paused. A file film showing the salon as it looked earlier with police cars and an ambulance out front, started to run. At the same time, B. J.'s voice, sounding as if it was recorded earlier, explained that the body was found by a patron of the salon during a busy afternoon. The stretcher bearing the body moved from the doorway to the ambulance in exactly the time it took for B. J. to deliver her explanation of the events.

"We'll be watching this case closely, John," she told the anchor in the studio, when the picture returned to live, "and we'll have an update at eleven."

"We look forward to it B. J.," said John, as he turned to another story.

Wally shook her head. "We're in for it again."

"And you're in the middle again," said Nate, grabbing her for another hug. He kissed the top of her head. "What am I going to do with you?"

Wally hoped that he was softening in his attitude. She didn't need another person making her walk on egg shells. Debbie, their sweet but high-strung daughter, at least of late, was enough for anyone.

Nate and Wally had just sat down to dinner when Debbie and Elliot bounced in giggling about the tailor in the tuxedo rental store. Elliot, looking somewhat red-faced, had taken off his suit jacket and his shirt collar was open. His curly light brown hair seemed a little damp from his exertions, and his dark blue eyes darted to the dinner table, as if counting the number of place settings.

Naturally, in Wally's house, there was plenty of food. Wally had made a dairy meal of cheese enchiladas, and had set the table for four, despite Debbie's assurances that they would not be there for dinner. Elliot was his usual hungry self. Debbie, slender as a blade of grass, wearing jeans and a tight tee shirt, worried as always about fitting into her wedding dress, merely picked at her dinner. Wally was sure that neither one saw what was on their plates, because they were too busy gazing at each other.

Later, as Debbie gave her parents a kiss goodbye, Wally noticed a tension in the air. She knew it was caused by the unspoken references to the murder. She also realized that even if there was no problem with discussing it, she wouldn't have wanted to. The thought of the body still made her sick, and she felt it was too close. She had, after all, seen the man moments before he was killed and in all likelihood his killer who did the dirty deed literally behind Wally's back.

She'd had a growing sensation all afternoon that the clunk she felt on the wall may have been part of a struggle and just maybe, if she had gone to investigate, she might have been able to prevent the murder.

"Are you all right?" asked Nate as he helped her clear the table after the young couple left. "I'm sorry I accused you of causing trouble."

Wally picked up Debbie's empty plate. "I'm afraid you might be right, though," she admitted. Without being able to stop them, she felt tears forming.

Nate stopped rinsing the dishes and came over to her. He took her in his arms and held her tightly until she calmed down. Then he listened to her concerns. By the time she was done he'd lost his nurturing look and had become speculative.

"As much as I hate to say this, you have to tell Elliot. You could help pinpoint the time of the assault. Didn't you say that the police said that they can tell the time of death but they can't tell if he died right away? That could mean he was attacked earlier, and other people might have been there at the time."

Wally nodded. "I guess so. But they're going to want to know more than just the time. They'll want to know what I heard and saw."

"So you'll tell them. The sooner you get it over with, the sooner you can get back to normal. Do you feel better now?"

"As a matter of fact, I do," said Wally. The thought of having to talk to the police about the murder again bothered her, as did the self-knowledge that as soon as the horror of it wore off she'd be chafing at the idea of helping to solve it. Unbidden, the bloody image floated back into her brain. She was not at the point of curiosity yet, just nausea. "I could use another hug."

* * *

The next morning, Elliot, Dominique, Ryan, the ever edgy Davis from Essex County and his partner, Brady, all descended on Resplendence Salon & Spa. They were there to finish their site inspection so the salon could open at 7:00, as requested by the owner.

Inspector Davis had been outraged by the Grosvenor mayor's decision to let the salon reopen. Less than twenty-four hours after the murder was too soon to allow all kinds of people to come through the scene of the crime, but Davis had been unable to obtain permission to keep the salon doors closed. The mayor had used the argument that at least thirty people had been there when it happened, and even if they had all left immediately, instead of finishing their beauty treatments, there would still have been the same problems with evidence.

So they had little time to work. It was to be Elliot's first official time in the salon, although not strictly his first visit. He had gone in there as a child with his mother, but that was before Logan bought it, acquired two additional adjoining storefronts, and made it the world-renowned spa that it allegedly was, at least according to its brochures. The advertising flyers available at the reception counter were pretty slick, as Davis had pointed out in his usual cynical these-people-have-too-much-money way. It made Elliot wonder again what kind of background the wiry detective from the county had.

There was little time to speculate, however, as they combed Consultation Room A in search of clues.

"Nothing in here has been touched, with the exception of the body and murder weapon," Dominique assured them as they made their way into the murder room. She looked fresh and bright, and her warm brown skin glowed notwithstanding the early morning hour. "The forensics people are positive that they have everything they could possibly need. They were here until eight o'clock last night, dusting for fingerprints and taking pictures. No one else has been in here."

Davis snorted. "Hmph."

"Can I have my crew clean it up then?" Logan asked. His

edgy voice was understandable to Elliot, considering the circumstances, as was his nervous way of bouncing on his toes. He was also sweating slightly under his open physician's jacket.

"No." Davis grumbled. "No matter what your mayor says, this room is going to be sealed." He turned to Dominique's partner, Ryan. "You. Get the tape."

Ryan hurried to do Davis's bidding, and returned holding the yellow crime scene tape in his hand like an offering.

"He looks like a puppy," Dominique whispered, loudly enough for Elliot to hear but no one else.

He hid a smile and stared at the room. The soft gray walls were papered in a delicate texture, with flecks of pink, green, and powder blue giving the impression of flowers. A perfect square, the room was eight feet on all sides, providing enough space for a black marble counter with a sink, a chair, and a closet.

There was plenty of blood left in the center of the room and on the chair, and smudges of it had dried on the counter. Elliot noticed that along with smudge marks, the wall without the counter had two black scuff marks. He started to move close to it, to get a better look.

"Stay away from there," Davis warned. "I don't want you prosecution boys mucking up the crime scene."

Elliot shook his head. Davis seemed to have forgotten that only yesterday he wanted Elliot in as a detective. "Look, you wanted me to . . ."

"Oh," said Davis, not hiding his chagrin, "that's right. Go ahead Mr. Big Mouth, Esquire. Just be careful."

Elliot edged closer to the mark. Dominique came up beside him. "I guess there's no way to know whether that mark means anything," she said.

"Logan might know. He might be able to tell us if it was there, or at least which cleaning person we could ask."

"Do you think it's important?"

"It might be."

Elliot turned to go out of the room and find the owner. He was feeling slightly claustrophobic anyway.

"Who came in here?" shouted Davis. Fingerprint dust all over the floor under the doorknob had a footprint in it. "Who did this?"

Ryan turned bright red. "Sorry sir. It happened last night. I leaned over too far and had to step in it to avoid falling."

"If you local pretend detectives can't keep yourself out of trouble, you can keep yourself out of this case."

"But Captain Jaeger said . . ."

Dominique put her hand on Ryan's arm. "Shh."

It was too late. Davis went into one of his routines about local police captains. Elliot and Dominique had heard it all before.

Elliot excused himself and followed Davis's partner Brady's broad rear out toward the back door to the salon. The walk over there was about seventy feet, and there was a turn at the last end, leaving the actual door and steps down to the parking obscured. Remnants of fingerprint powder flecked the floor on both sides of the door, which had been sealed at some point after the murder. Elliot consulted his notes and saw that it wasn't until at least a half hour after the discovery of the body that the door was sealed off.

That was the good news. The bad was that the front door hadn't been sealed off until hours later because clients were still being groomed. No amount of police muscle had been able to move them out of the salon until after their makeovers had been completed. Even Tillie Morris, Elliot's future grandmother-in-law, had refused to go until after her comb-out and thorough lacquering.

Brady seemed satisfied with his inspection of the doorway, and went back into the waiting room of the salon. Elliot went around the other way, through the main work area, to get a sense of how the murderer might have gone through the room. With enough distraction it was possible, he supposed, to be unnoticed, provided the person wasn't totally out of place.

Just after 7:00 a teenage girl roared her expensive sports car past the salon and, with brakes squealing, headed for the parking lot. As soon as she got out of her car, she ran to the back door, wearing the shortest, tightest shorts Elliot had ever seen, and a midriff-exposing tee shirt. She was not one of those skinny teens. She was rounded appropriately, even amply, and was perfectly put together, except for her blond-highlighted brown hair, which hung in wet strings around her head.

She shrieked curses and pounded her fists on the locked back door, after which two minutes of silence were a prelude to her storming into the front of the salon.

"What idiot locked that back door?" she screamed. "I don't have time to walk all the way around to the front." No one responded, which did not stop her diatribe. "It's hot out," she whined. "My makeup is absolutely sliding off. Now what am I going to do?"

Logan went over to the girl, a big smile nervously plastered on his face. "Roxanna, darling. Don't fret. I'm sorry about the door. It couldn't be helped. Didn't you hear what happened?"

"No. What do I care if something happened?" The girl looked at Logan with contempt, as if to say that if something didn't affect her, it was insignificant. Elliot, who had been watching the entire exchange with amusement, was reminded of several obnoxious high school classmates. That this girl was here to have her hair blown and styled before she put in an appearance at school made him appreciate his own down-to-earth Debbie all the more. She was still torn about having her hair and make-up done professionally on the day of their wedding. She was so beautiful anyway, it probably wouldn't matter.

"Nothing that you need to concern yourself with," Logan told Roxanna. "Just sit in your usual seat and I'll do your hair. We don't want you to be late for school."

The girl seemed to accept Logan's absence of explanation. She sat quietly looking through a magazine while he blew her hair dry, combed, teased and sprayed it. The latest fashion statement hairstyle looked reminiscent of something worn by one of the stars of the hottest TV sitcom and didn't seem all that complicated to do, but Roxanna, whose Dad was undoubtedly very wealthy, seemed content to have Logan do it for her, just as she was apparently happy to have someone do her nails for her. The acrylic tips on her fingers were studded with tiny rhinestones, which Roxanna compared with the nail polish ads in the magazine. Elliot wondered what Davis, with his well known low opinion of wealthy people and their spoiled children, would say if he knew.

But it didn't seem as if he'd find out because Roxanna was gone before Davis came out of the consultation room. Dominique accompanied him, with Ryan tagging behind. The red-haired detective hung on every word that Davis said, as if they were handed down by God to Moses.

"This would be the outside of that wall," said Davis, checking the measurements that showed on the carpenter's measuring tape he had trailing behind him. He looked at Elliot. "Those black marks you noticed were on the other side over here."

Elliot didn't mention that he was standing there because he had figured that out. What he was doing now was trying to determine what that might mean. Davis's derogatory attitude did not merit a response, however, so Elliot kept quiet. He also didn't mention that he had just asked Logan, after his client left, if he knew whether the marks were new. Logan had gone around to the room to see if he could tell, taking the long route so that he could toss the comb he'd used to tease Roxanna's hair into a tall glass jar filled with blue solution.

"The marks are definitely new," Logan said to Elliot, when he returned. He seemed to be unclear who was in charge of the investigation, so he answered Elliot's question directly to him.

"Are you at it again?" asked Davis. A tiny hint of a smile showed that Davis realized Elliot was ahead of him on the scuff question but the scowl of his dark eyebrows indicated clearly that he still did not fully consider Elliot to be on the same team.

Dominique, covering her mouth with her long slim fingers, turned a giggle into a cough.

"So what, if anything, did you figure out?" Davis asked.

"It's hard to say, but if someone in this area," Elliot indicated a four foot space, "happened to be listening, he or she might have heard something."

"Did anyone mention that on your questionnaire?" Davis asked Dominique.

"I don't remember seeing anything like that, but we will be questioning people again, and we'll ask about it."

"Are you through here?" asked Logan.

"Not quite," said Davis. "But you can let the uglies in now. We'll try to stay out of your way."

Logan sniffed in an offended manner and walked away. It was nearly 7:30. Elliot left to get some coffee with Dominique, grateful that Ryan stayed with Davis and his partner. For a few minutes, it would be back to old times.

Dominique led the way to the same seat she always chose when she and Elliot went to the diner. It faced the sidewalk so she could see who passed by. Elliot had nearly as good a view through the mirror on the opposite wall. His view was only second best, but Elliot had long ago given up trying to outmaneuver his former partner.

Based on what she told him of her life with James, her husband was outclassed too. Of course, Dominique never said anything so blatant, but James's dental office seemed to be the only place he was in charge. Considering his own upcoming marital merger, it made sense. Tough, strong women were worth it—he hoped.

"James is singing the baby blues again," Dom said, sipping an iced tea. "His sister just had twins. Now everyone is looking at me for a repeat performance."

"You're supposed to have twins?"

Dominique laughed. "No, I think one would be enough. But one would also be the minimum, and soon."

Elliot tried to be as neutral as possible when he asked the next question. In a way, and even though it wasn't his business, he was on James's side. A baby was a wonderful prospect, and he hoped that he and Debbie wouldn't have to wait too long. "How do you feel about it?"

Leaning forward, Dominique whispered, "I'd like to. But I

have to figure out when. I don't want someone else telling me I'm ready."

"So I guess you aren't."

"Not this week, anyway," Dominique said. "I have to solve this murder case."

"You mean we."

"If you say so."

Her eyes twinkled, but Elliot felt challenged nevertheless. He knew she'd love to ace him out of this. They were no longer working on the same team. The goal may have been the same, but it was every man for himself.

Dominique pulled out three dollars and left them on the table as she stood up. "I'll see you at the funeral."

Chapter Five

Wally unloaded three bags of groceries from the trunk of her car and somehow, with great agility, managed to carry them into Tillie's apartment building. Two residents of the Jewish retirement facility saw her coming and, after a short argument, one of them pulled open the door.

"We really aren't supposed to do this," one elderly woman apologized, ignoring the glares of her companion. "We'd get in trouble if anyone saw us."

"I appreciate it," said Wally, straining to keep the bags upright.

The other woman spoke up. "They're being strict again because of the robbery."

Wally had heard about the resident who was mugged. The management of the building had decided that since the woman had her identification along with her keys in her purse they would have to change all the locks. Visitors were not to be allowed in unless a resident was there to vouch for them. Luckily, many of the residents knew Wally by sight.

As she walked toward the elevator, she hoped that the women would notice that she couldn't ring for it because of the bundles she carried. Unfortunately, they were locked in another battle.

"Robbery, schmobbery," said her companion. "Wally here was at the murder. Now that's important!"

With her nose, Wally rang for the elevator herself. "Say hello to your darling mother-in-law," one of the ladies called to Wally's back as the door opened and she wondered how she'd indicate which floor she wanted. "Tell her we'll bring her mail later."

Tillie managed to get the door to her apartment open before Wally got to it, even with her cast. "I saw your car," she said, holding it wide enough for Wally to pass. "What took you so long to come upstairs?"

"The meet and greet committee," Wally explained.

"Oh, Ida and Rose. They talk a lot, and never get anything done."

Unpacking the bags, Wally handed things to her mother-in-law to put away.

Tillie shook her head after squeezing the pears. "Leave them on the counter for a few days." She picked up the package of strawberries, depositing it on the top shelf of her refrigerator. "Ida and Rose know everyone's business," Tillie said, returning to the subject, "and although they fight with each other, they get along with most other people, surprisingly."

Wally knew that there were many people in the building who didn't get along with anyone, and there were several nasty cliques, as bad as any in junior high schools today. On the other hand, she knew that Tillie got along with everyone and was quite sought after, particularly by the mah-jongg, canasta, and Rummy-q groups.

Tillie put away the milk. "The funny thing is, they're sisters-in-law. But they always fight. The caterwauling can get loud sometimes."

Wally hoped she never had to see that.

"Did they mention the murder?" Tillie asked.

"Yes," said Wally. "One of them, I don't know who is who, mentioned that mugging when she let me in, and the other one said that the murder was more important."

"That's all anyone is talking about these days. They have asked me what happened about a million times. Don't look at me that way, it isn't because they keep forgetting that they asked. At least not all of them . . ." Her voice trailed off into a giggle.

Wally hadn't been aware of looking at Tillie any particular way. In fact, she'd been concentrating on emptying the grocery bags.

"Haven't the police caught the murderer yet?" Tillie asked, her tone more serious. "I would have thought they'd catch him right away."

"Him? Why do you say him?"

"I just assumed."

"So you think it was one of the male hairdressers?"

Tillie shook her head. "No, I didn't say that."

"There weren't that many other men in the place, as I recall. And I would think a man would stand out."

"Oh, come on," Tillie chided, "and get with the twenty-first century already, dear. Many men go to the spa for a haircut and some even get a manicure."

Wally had to laugh at her eighty-three year old mother-in-law telling her to get with it. "I didn't see any male clients there that morning; did you?"

"You know I was under one contraption or another the whole time."

Wally nodded. "But I wasn't, and I didn't notice any men getting anything done that day."

"What did Elliot say?" Tillie was beyond proud of her soon to be grandson-in-law. "He'll probably solve this in no time."

"He's asking questions like the other detectives."

"For this he went to law school?"

"It's complicated, but this is the way his boss wants it."

"So what did he say?"

"He had me look over the list. It helped me remember more people I has seen, but nothing indicated who might have done it."

"Why do you look so worried?"

"I'm afraid that it might interfere with the wedding."

"Oh, no," said Tillie, with complete confidence in her voice, "they'll be understanding."

Wally didn't want to burst Tillie's bubble, but Elliot's boss was not that type of understanding guy. In fact, he'd already told Elliot that until the case was solved, he could consider himself to have no outside life.

Elliot arrived at the cemetery shortly before the funeral procession. It was one of those spring days that warns of a potentially hot summer. He politely stayed out of the way of the grieving family, or families, depending on how one looked at the three ex-wives, and their daughters. From the research he had done so far, he knew that Garth did not have living parents, or any siblings. He guessed, based on who showed up and the simple grave side service, that he had no other relatives either, although it was possible, based on what Elliot had learned, that he had alienated all of them by asking for loans.

Dominique and her partner, who had given him that information, were also at the cemetery, but Inspector Davis and his partner, Brady, were absent. Dominique explained that Davis, in his own disparaging way, had decided that they could handle the observation on their own. Elliot didn't tell them that Davis had said the same thing to him.

The three ex-wives were as different as they could be. The middle ex, Sally, arrived by limousine in heavy widow's attire, entirely covered in expensive black clothing, which made her look overheated. Considering how overweight she was, it was scary to think of her wearing all that dark material on such a hot day. Beside her was Madeline, around ten, also wearing an expensive black dress. Her round face was uncovered, and her eyes had a narrow, calculating look. Elliot concluded that either she didn't fully understand her father's death or, for some reason, she was not devastated by it.

The other child, Lisa, daughter of the third wife, was about six-years-old, and seemed bewildered. Dominique gasped when she saw the teary, wide-eyed, thin, girl in the simple and somewhat too small dress.

"She's so young to be going through this," Dominique said, her voice cracking. Ryan, standing beside her, was silent, sniffling. He held his bottom jaw jutting out, to match his ramrod straight spine, but his eyes betrayed his emotions. Elliot felt sorry for him. He'd have to develop a thicker skin.

Lisa's mother, Tess, wore a simple dark t-dress. She was younger than the other exes, and appeared to be less upset than Sally, but not as happy as Rita, the first ex.

Rita, the first Mrs. Garth Barkley, stood at the grave, looking at the casket. She wore a short, dark blue dress revealing well-toned calves, and her shoulder length, brown hair cascaded over her face when she lowered it. Elliot had the distinct impression that she did that to hide laughter.

There were several other people in attendance. Logan Fletcher, of course, wearing a suit instead of his physician's jacket, as well as most of the people from the salon, and from what Elliot remembered of his witness list, many people whose hair Garth styled. They were not all sad looking. A look of grim triumph passed across several faces.

But Sally's sobs drowned out the sounds of mirth that were strangely frequent at the funeral. As the preacher intoned over the casket, seeming to be in search of kind words, people exchanged smiles. Three women chuckled aloud when the preacher said of Garth, "A man whose services were sought after by many." Logan, with his hands clasped behind his back, bounced slightly on his toes, before catching himself, clearing his throat and placing his legs further apart while looking reverently at the ground.

Sally had to be helped back into the waiting limousine by people whose obvious opinions of her loss did not match her own grief. When the other ex-wives returned to their own cars, Rita to a Jetta, and Tess with little Lisa, to a beat up old Saturn, the only people left at the cemetery were the grave workers and law enforcement people. There didn't seem to be any point in lingering, as no one was actually dancing on the grave, so Elliot left.

Back in his cubicle, Elliot wondered how one man, Garth Barkley, a hairdresser, could have been involved in so many different ventures. While Elliot couldn't imagine himself setting, cutting, styling, coloring, perming and blow drying anyone's hair for a living, he doubted that he would have felt the need to do so much else to get his mind off it.

For starters, and not the most glaring departure from simple hairstyling, Garth was a part owner in Logan's salon. He had not invested at the outset, nor just prior to any of the many renovations. In fact, there was no record of any capital investment by Garth at all. It seemed that his ownership suddenly popped up on paper one day. Elliot made a note to check on the circumstances.

Still, it made sense for a hairdresser to have a part ownership in the salon where he worked, as did the secrecy. The reason for the concealment might be as simple as wanting tips from the tightwads who felt that a salon owner should not be tipped like a regular operator.

In an oddly related incident, Garth had somehow managed to bring a lawsuit down on the head of Logan. Garth had pictures of a young woman with a particularly terrific haircut surrounding her pretty face blown up and put on buses with Logan's salon's name and phone number underneath. As it turned out, no one at the salon had been responsible for that haircut; the woman had never even set foot in Grosvenor, let alone the salon. Court documents named a photography studio that, surprisingly enough, Garth was also associated with, as co-defendant in the lawsuit. They had taken the picture of the plaintiff at her request, but not for the purpose of any kind of advertising.

Elliot looked at the name of the photo studio and decided that it might be useful to make a phone call to them, just to see if they had any knowledge of Garth's activities prior to his death. He pulled out his copy of the suburban Essex County phone book, looked up the number in Livingston, and called.

"Perfect Image," said a man's voice. "We are temporarily away from the office. Please leave a message." A long beep followed. Elliot did not leave a message. He picked up his jacket, edged out from behind his desk, and escaped from his cubicle. He was eager to be out on the road again.

* * *

Crystal Garrick knew that she should tell the police what she knew about Garth, but she didn't want to hurt anyone or get anyone into trouble. As receptionist at the salon, she had fielded numerous angry phone calls for the dead man, both from business partners in his various ventures, and from distraught women. Without fail in every case, Garth told her to take a number. He couldn't interrupt his work with his clients for a phone call. Even if he was not busy, he said the same thing, so Crystal had little regard for his excuses. He was 'a troublemaker, that one,' as her grandmother used to say.

For that reason, she had not been all that surprised that he was found dead, just surprised about where.

The police, knowing that she had a clear view of most of the salon and that it was her job to keep track of all the people present at any given time, had already questioned her several times about whom she saw that afternoon. She had told them truthfully that it seemed as if she saw just about anyone who had ever come in there, because the place had been that crowded. She knew she'd signed for at least seven deliveries and that the water delivery had come, because it was over a half hour late. The man's delay raised the eyebrows on the police officer who was questioning her, but it had been easily explained. The water delivery man had said that he'd been installing a new system at the real estate company down the street. That had been confirmed, along with an embarrassed admission that the local realtors were no longer willing to submit prospective clients to the foul tasting tap water emanating from the faucets of Grosvenor. Crystal had gotten a good laugh out of that one. "Let them find out after they buy the house, huh?" she'd said to the frazzled woman from the agency.

Since the police were using her desk as a home base on the afternoon of the murder, Crystal had a whole new insight into many of the people whom she had worked with and seen in town over the two year period since she came to the spa. It had been an education.

There had been some strangers there that afternoon, such

as the heating and cooling repairmen who had been called in when the air conditioning went on the fritz. Luckily most of the customers, except possibly those under the hair dryers, had remained comfortable while they were there, because the back door had been propped open to let a fresh breeze in. Possibly it had let someone else in, someone with less pure motives than the spring air.

It was too bad that Crystal could not see that back door from her counter area. She might have seen who came in with a sinister present for Garth. A shiver went down her spine. In all likelihood, she did see the person. Probably many people did.

Crystal knew that one of the witnesses, Wally Morris, who had been present but not occupied during the time of the murder because she was waiting for her mother-in-law, had earned a reputation for solving murders. She was able to work behind the scenes with the police, probably because of her soon-to-be son-in-law, the really cute prosecutor. Crystal looked forward to visiting with her.

Chapter Six

A sign on the door of Perfect Image told Elliot that the studio was closed until further notice. A phone number, the same one that Elliot had dialed earlier, was printed below with the recommendation that any bride or other concerned party should call and leave a message which would receive prompt and immediate attention. That seemed unlikely, as a fire had burned there recently and police caution tape crisscrossed the entryway.

The interior of the studio was in a shambles. Elliot doubted that anyone who had been waiting for pictures would ever get them. It looked as if the fire had spread to the photo vaults, as well as the studio space. The plate glass window had been cracked, not enough to replace with plywood or Elliot wouldn't have been able to see inside, just enough to require duct tape to hold it together.

He drove over to the Livingston police station, explained who he was, and asked the desk sergeant what had happened, and most importantly when. It turned out that the damage had been done the evening of Garth Barkley's murder.

"Where can I reach the owner?" Elliot asked.

"He skipped. I don't really blame him. I wouldn't give two cents for his life after those brides find out their pictures are gone, or the other ones find out he won't be there to photograph their weddings."

Elliot winced. Maybe he'd better take a minute to check with Debbie and see which photographer they would be using.

He forced himself back to the case. "If he turns up, would you have one of the detectives call me?"

"Sure. We'll call you right away. I don't think he'll last long enough for you to question him otherwise."

The gossip mills had already ground up the news about the photography studio by the time Wally got home from the nursery school. They had not only ground it up, they had spit it out, right into the laps of anyone known to be planning an affair in the near future, such as the Morrises. Phone messages and calls abounded, from close relations to well wishers who generally did not communicate with the recipients of those phone calls. The calls had been remarkably similar in content and syrupy sweetness of delivery, most simply made to confirm that the Morris wedding had not planned to use Perfect Image.

Wally's favorite, so to speak, had come from Denise Kaplan. "Wally, how are you holding up?" the voice had said as soon as Wally answered the phone, which she'd had to run into the house to do since she was out walking Sammy.

Gasping for breath, Wally had stammered, "I'm fine, and you?" hoping that the person would somehow reveal who she was during the ensuing answer without Wally having to ask.

"Oh, just fine," the anonymous caller had answered. "Brett got wonderful grades from Harvard, and Roger and I are so proud."

Mystery solved, thought Wally. Denise, the biggest braggart in town, was on the phone. The only question was why?

Denise's repetition of her initial question provided a clue. "How are you coping with this photography thing? You've heard about Perfect Image, haven't you? Well, if you didn't, let me tell you . . ."

"I heard all about it. We weren't planning to use them, so you don't have to worry."

"I didn't think you were," said Denise, barely losing stride in her end of the conversation and completely disregarding Wally's interruption. "They were so expensive, you know."

Wally didn't respond to the insinuation that her spending habits were frugal. Denise was not someone she had ever in her life confided in, nor was she someone whom Wally thought it important to impress. The implication that she did not buy the best was clear enough, even if, in Wally's opinion, it was erroneous.

"So how do you feel?" asked Denise.

"About that studio going out of business? I can't honestly say it upsets me."

"Are you sure you aren't repressing your anxiety?" Denise asked, giving evidence to her years of seeing an analyst.

"About what? It doesn't concern me."

"Are you sure?"

"Yes."

"You should call whoever you signed a contract with, just to make sure."

"Make sure of what?"

"Make sure they aren't going to dump you to work for someone else. You know, those people who had signed with Perfect Image are likely to give them more money and they might decide to go for it."

Wally thought that extremely unlikely. Denise made it sound as if she'd contracted with some fly-by-night outfit. But she wasn't about to get upset. Too many people in town had been annoyed by things Denise Kaplan had said for Wally to be one of them.

"You know," she said, "I'll look into it. Thanks so much for warning me. I'd love to talk with you, and really catch up. But as you can guess, I really must make this other call now."

Denise was all solicitousness. "Yes, of course. I understand. Good luck."

Wally hung up, worn out from restraining her tongue. Her first thought was to call Louise and have a 'can-you-believe-that-woman?' session, but of course, most frustratingly, Louise was on vacation in Hawaii.

With fifteen craft kits to put together for her four-year-old class, Wally brought empty coffee cans up from the basement, along with some felt and a bag of googly eyes. Sitting down to work cutting the felt into different shapes, she found her mind wandering.

Her dialing finger itched. She wanted more than anything to call someone and tell her how annoying Denise had been, even more catty than usual since she knew she wasn't invited to the wedding. It occurred to Wally that a quick call to check on her mother-in-law might be in order and would give her the opportunity to vent. With each passing minute she was becoming more overdue.

Tillie answered on the first ring. "Thank goodness it's you," she said, when she'd heard Wally's voice.

"Is something wrong?"

"Not exactly, or at least, not any more than there usually is around here. It depends whose side you are on."

"Whose side of what?"

"The latest dispute."

Wally counted up the blue strips of felt. "What is this one about?"

"You won't believe it."

Wally thought about that. It usually was not worth finding out what some of the ladies in Tillie's building were fighting about, because it often was too ridiculous for words. But Denise's phone call had put her into a strangely adversarial mood and she felt like hearing about the argument. "Let's hear it."

"You'll be sorry. But here goes. You remember Zeta? She sat at our dinner table."

There was assigned seating in the apartment dining room to avoid constant squabbles. Wally didn't blame the management one bit. The seniors could be as immature as the four-year-olds in her class. "Yes."

"Well, I don't know if I told you this, but she died on Sunday morning."

"I'm sorry to hear that."

"It happens around here sometimes."

Quite a lot, actually, Wally thought. But she didn't point that out to Tillie.

"Muriel," Tillie continued, "the other woman at our table, was her good friend. They spent a lot of time together."

Picking up the red felt, Wally said, "Is she taking it very hard?"

Tillie chuckled. "You decide. Muriel went to the office on Monday morning, before the funeral, and requested that Sadie sit with us from now on."

"Why did she do that?"

"Let me tell you it wasn't because she missed Zeta, but because she was afraid that one of the less cognitive people would be assigned."

"Less cognitive?"

"You know which ones."

Wally knew. There were a few, not many, just a few, of the people in Tillie's building who had a hard time with their memories. On several occasions, Wally herself had been berated for failing to visit one of them, because she had been mistaken for someone's neglectful daughter. It unnerved her, but there were usually so many of the other residents around that they helped her out of the situation.

"So then what happened?" Wally asked, while she slipped the red felt triangles into a plastic bag.

"Well, some of the ladies decided that Muriel did a terrible thing to Zeta by asking for Sadie to join the table before Zeta was cold in her grave. They're saying nasty things about her, and that's making her feel worse than Zeta's death did."

Wally wasn't sure what to think about the whole thing. As much as she loved Tillie, she wasn't going to declare her own opinion until she was sure how Tillie felt. "What do you think?"

"You sound like a psychologist."

"Sorry," said Wally, remembering how annoying Denise's pseudo-psychoanalysis was. "Whose side are you on?"

"I'm not on anybody's side. Do you think I'm crazy? I just keep my mouth shut. Actually, it isn't a bad thing. Sadie has her own teeth, so we won't have to worry about any bizarre events during dinner."

The scissors slipped out of Wally's hand. "What?"

"Dentures don't stay in that well on some people. One good sneeze and . . ."

Feeling a slight sense of revulsion, Wally picked up the scissors. The discussion of teeth and dentures had to be one of her least favorite topics, so she changed the subject. She told Tillie about the phone call she'd had from Denise. Tillie was tickled.

By the time the call ended Wally felt freed of her annoyance. She got up to make herself a cup of tea.

Before the kettle boiled, however, the phone rang again. Wally braced herself.

The question was as expected, "Did you hear about the photography studio?" but the caller was a surprise. It was Elliot.

"Yes, I did. Why?"

"I just wanted to be sure that's not the photographer we picked."

Wally laughed inwardly at his illusion that he had made any choices or that he had any control over the wedding, but she wasn't about to burst his bubble. "No, it isn't."

She could hear his sigh of relief. "Thank goodness."

"How did you hear about it?" asked Wally. "I thought you were buried in the murder case. Is there a connection?"

"I'm not sure I can explain the whole thing," said Elliot.

"I understand. Whatever."

"Mrs., uh, Wally?" said Elliot uncomfortably. The jury was still out on what he would ultimately call her and Nate. Adam, Rachel's husband, called them Mom and Dad. But that didn't mean that Elliot had to as well.

"What?"

"Who are you and what have you done with my future mother-in-law?"

Wally laughed. "What do you mean?"

"Is that really you? Or have you been possessed by aliens?"

"I'm too busy to get involved in your case, other than to answer your questions. Just do your job and get it solved before the wedding."

"Aren't you even going to ask how it's going?"

"You obviously have leads," said Wally. "I'm sure you'll get the killer." She hung up, hoping she sounded suitably confident, but puzzled by the tiny feeling that there was something she was supposed to discuss with Elliot about the case. Since the wedding was looming closer each day and she had made a promise to stay out of the investigation, even though it was interesting, she put all thoughts of involvement out of her mind.

"I had a strange call today," said Nate, as he washed his hands before dinner. They were having lamb chops, which were smoking on the grill outside the kitchen door, and the breeze coming through the screens smelled wonderful.

"Only one?" said Wally. "You're lucky."

Nate gave her one of his quizzical looks, but didn't ask her what she meant. His own face said something to the effect that he was sure she'd tell him, sooner or later. "Elliot called."

Wally, with pot-mittened hands, pulled the baked potatoes out of the oven. "And . . .", she said in a way she hoped was leading, as she popped them onto a serving dish.

"And he seemed to think there was something strange about you. Naturally I congratulated him on finally noticing just how strange you are."

"Oh," Wally giggled, "you."

"Me what?" he said innocently. His blue eyes sparkled playfully. "Seriously though, he wondered why you weren't giving him the third degree on the case."

Wally drained the vegetables and put them on the table. "Truthfully? I didn't know Garth, or any of the people involved, so I don't feel the same compulsion I did before. Plus, I just don't have time."

"We should be grateful for little things, I guess," he said, under his breath.

"What are you mumbling?" Wally said. Then, to prove that she'd heard every word, "I can't believe you think that this wedding, on top of everything else I do, is a little thing."

Nate stopped her from running around the kitchen long enough to wrap his long arms around her. Looking down from so far above her, he smiled. "You're doing a terrific job, just like the last time. Don't worry so much." Disengaging himself, he picked up the long meat fork and a plate. "Hold the dog when I come in," he called, over his shoulder. "I'm not inclined to share my dinner with him tonight."

Wally looked at Sammy, who slept soundly, with his legs twitching in his dreams. He didn't seem likely to try to knock the food out of Nate's hand this evening, but all the same, she stood between the dog and the door when Nate came back. Sammy had a bad reputation, deservedly so.

As they ate, Wally filled him in on her phone call to the photographer. It had taken an extraordinary amount of chutzpah on her part to call him, because she knew it would be insulting, but at the same time she hated the niggling feeling she was getting as a result of Denise's phone call. So she contrived a need to speak to him about some more pictures that she had suddenly decided had to be taken. The extra few hundred dollars they would now have to spend, just because Wally couldn't be honest with the photographer, would probably haunt her for days.

For his part, Nate was considerate enough to let her think he wasn't annoyed. He even went so far as to say that it would probably be a good idea to get those pictures taken.

"What else did Elliot have to say for himself?" Nate asked, cutting his lamb chop. "I had another call and couldn't talk to him any more. Did he tell you about the case?"

She explained to her husband about the relationship of the burnt-out photography studio to the dead hairdresser. A pensive look filled his face. "Have you told Elliot about the bump on the wall?"

"No!" An unpleasant perspiration broke out on Wally's neck at having forgotten. "That's what I forgot, while I was trying so hard to stay out of it."

Elliot picked up the phone on the second ring.

"Hi," said Wally, for some reason feeling shy.

"Don't tell me that the photographer canceled," said Elliot.

"No, I told you everything was okay. It's just that I forgot to tell you something kind of important."

"Are my parents going to be annoyed?"

"What? Oh, no. It isn't about the wedding."

"Well, if it isn't about the wedding, then . . . is it about the murder?"

"I've always said you were smart."

"I thought that was for falling in love with your daughter."

Wally resisted the urge to continue the verbal sparring. "I have some information, something I should have told you earlier. See, while I was waiting for Tillie to get done with one of the phases of her perm, I was leaning on a wall. I'm pretty sure that it was the outside of the consultation room." She took a deep breath.

"And . . . ?"

"I felt a bump, like a push against the wall, from the other side. I was worried for a second that it was too thin and whoever was on the other side would break through, especially when it happened again. And now I think that it might have been during the attack on Garth."

"What? Really? Do you by any chance know that exact time?"

Wally felt her face burn and was glad that Elliot couldn't see her. "Well, I did look at my watch and wonder if I had time for an errand."

Elliot sounded excited. "And it was what time?"

"One thirty-six. My watch is digital."

"Thanks. Wait. Is there anything else?"

"No, I promise. I feel so stupid for not telling you sooner."

"Chalk it up to too much on your mind. Don't worry about it."

But Wally did, then, and for the rest of the evening.

Chapter Seven

Dominique rapped on the windows of Elliot's car and waited while he lowered the driver's window. "Do you have time to talk?" she asked, looking over her shoulder.

"Yes," said Elliot. "Do you want to talk in the car, or can we go somewhere for a cup of coffee?"

"What's the matter, too hot out here for you?" Dominique asked derisively. But the beads of perspiration on her nose told Elliot that she agreed. He followed her to the diner, anxiously awaiting the chilly blast of air at the doorway. No matter how much he turned up his car air conditioner, it was no match for the heat and humidity that day.

The unusually hot spring weather had forced many people to seek relief in the diner. It was fairly crowded for midmorning and the waitresses who would normally have stood around sucking on their cigarettes at that time of day were running all over with glasses of iced tea and iced coffee. Luckily, school was still in session, and Elliot and Dominique were able to get a booth in the back of the restaurant.

"You seem to have a great deal on your mind," said Elliot. "Spill it."

"You don't seem to have much patience," Dominique observed. "What's eating you?"

"Have you checked the calendar lately? The wedding is

only three and a half weeks away and so far we don't even have a suspect."

Dominique put her dark hand with its long slender fingers onto Elliot's. "Calm down. It isn't that we don't have a suspect. It's that we have several and no clear favorite."

"This isn't a horse race," said Elliot sourly.

Dominique smiled. "Too bad. I was just going to ask who Mrs. Morris had her money on."

"Not funny. She's staying out of it."

"That's a shame. She could probably help."

"Could we get back to what you wanted to talk to me about?"

"How much have you found out about Garth's private life? I mean, beside his three ex-wives?"

Elliot didn't need to consult his notes to answer that. "He had a few girlfriends. They were all married, and there's a good chance he was extorting, shall we say, gifts from them. Do you think one of them killed him?"

"It certainly is a possibility."

"None of them was seen at the salon that morning."

Dominique sighed. "Don't be so sure. We've already established, through actual trials, that someone could go in there, maybe go into the back and wait for Garth to come by, talk to him, and convince him to go into the consultation room. That person could commit the murder and leave, all without anyone knowing, except for the banging on the wall that Mrs. Morris heard and felt."

Elliot had told her the previous evening about Mrs. Morris's revelations. Dominique had taken the news much better than Davis did and did not blame Elliot for the delay. Davis had actually threatened to tell Elliot's boss that he was obstructing justice. Although the idea was absurd and Elliot knew he wouldn't, the thought still made him angry.

Dominique took a sip of water from her glass which was dripping with condensation. "It really is too bad that she didn't go investigate. We wouldn't have a mystery if she did."

"Or," said Elliot, "she could be dead. I'm just as glad that she didn't go see what was going on."

"Right. Okay, so we have those suspects. Several of them, plus the ex-wives, to whom he was not paying the court-ordered child support even though he made unexplained deposits into his account."

"Only two had children with him. The other one wasn't supposed to get anything."

"That's what she says. We can probably eliminate the exes, provided he didn't do anything to them just before he was bumped off and if their alibis hold up."

"Nice way to talk." Elliot scowled. "Very professional."

Dominique giggled. "I think my partner is wearing off on me."

"Where is the little twerp?"

"Do I detect jealousy?"

"Not really. Hostility maybe."

"What do you have against him?"

"He's like Eddie Haskell. Always kissing up to Davis."

"It has its advantages."

Elliot raised an eyebrow. But, looking at his watch, he decided to drop the discussion of Ryan in favor of returning to the case. "There are more suspects besides those women. Have you seen the weird kid with the body piercings?"

"Dakota. What about him?"

"From what I understand, his job is to stock the towels, sweep, do the wash, and clean up after the customers. He could be anywhere in the salon at any time."

"True. And if he had something against Garth, he could have done it and no one would ever notice that he wasn't where he should be. I'll check into it."

"Good," said Elliot. "Now, what about Logan?"

Dominique smiled. "That was what I wanted to tell you about. The salon was being sued because of something that Garth did and Logan was hopping mad. Maybe he's our guy."

"Another offensive haircut?" asked Elliot, referring to what Mrs. Morris had said about Garth's attempt to correct nature's mistakes with a style alteration.

"Not exactly. This has to do with a woman whose picture Garth plastered on buses all over Essex County with the name of the salon underneath. The use of the picture was completely unauthorized."

"I know about that. That was how I learned about that photo studio. Garth had a piece of the studio too, did you know that?"

Her eyes registered the ramifications. "So he took a picture of someone who looked good and used it to advertise the salon. How very upstanding of him."

"I get the sense," said Elliot, "that Garth did not feel that rules of ethics, courtesy or law applied to him."

"That's probably why someone was impelled to kill him." Dominique toyed with the wrapper of her straw. "Many of the people I talked to seemed to believe the killer did society a favor."

"People actually said that?"

Dominique made a face. "Well, no. It was just a feeling I got." She sipped some more of her water. "Do you think we should talk to the woman whose photograph Garth used without permission?"

"I already did, briefly," said Elliot. "She has an alibi. She was in New York at an antique show all day. We verified it with several colleagues."

"We have to keep digging," said Dominique soberly. "There may be many rocks to look under. We don't want to arrest the wrong person."

Elliot narrowed his eyes in an involuntary wince. "You mean not again."

"Um, hm. And besides, there's still Logan. It could have cost him the salon if he lost that suit."

"Don't tell me he won."

Dominique put up her hand. "Before you go into another tirade about juries, you should know that the case has been adjourned as the plaintiff's attorney is on maternity leave. No new trial date has been set. Not yet, anyway."

"Maybe Logan thought he'd better cut his losses by cutting Garth's life short."

"So you think he did it."

"He's high on my list."

"Is anyone else up there?"

Elliot weighed his loyalties. On the one hand he had known and worked with Dominique for years and trusted her with his life. On the other, the prosecutor's office had made it perfectly clear that the county was to be responsible for solving the case. Yet, if he didn't share with Dominique, he might miss important information. If he did, she could get the jump on him. It wouldn't be the first time.

So Elliot was left wondering how much to say. And the set of Dominique's shoulders said that suddenly, she was wondering, too.

Chapter Eight

Without looking up, Crystal knew there was someone standing in front of her. Her position as receptionist put her largely in charge of directing traffic at the spa, but also meant that as front line representative, she was the one-person meet and greet committee. She was also the one who had to answer the phone, book appointments, and determine, based on a new client's vague descriptions, what would be necessary to please her as a client and which hairdresser would be the best to provide it.

This morning was particularly busy, because they had to shuffle all of Garth's appointments and get them reassigned, at least those that weren't canceled. It was also a Wednesday, and more than the usual deliveries were due.

Because of this, Crystal was unable to look up just at the moment that a woman came to stand in front of the reception counter. She was busy signing for a delivery and thumbing through the appointment book looking for an opening with Jordan. She could tell, though, from what she could see out of the corner of her eyes, that the woman was thin, not terribly wealthy, at least based on her clothes, and nervous. That last factor puzzled Crystal, and she made an effort to speed up the decision making process of the woman on the phone.

She looked at the woman to reassure her she would be taken

care of soon and realized it was Tess Barkley. In an instant, she knew the reason for the nervousness.

"Tess," said Crystal, when she had finally ended the call. "I'm like, so sorry." Wondering whether that was the correct emotion to express to the last ex-wife of Garth, Crystal studied her for her reaction. She needed clues. When Sally had called, Logan had spent several valuable hours soothing her, and when Rita had called he'd had to promise to go out for a drink of champagne with her, to celebrate Garth's death. Crystal considered that totally gross and she didn't know whether Rita was serious, just that she wasn't sad. Now she was faced with Tess, whom she knew personally since this ex-wife of Garth had worked in the salon before the divorce. Crystal waited for her response.

"Thanks, I guess," said Tess. "Look, can I talk to you?"

Crystal looked at the work piling up, the phone ringing on three different lines, and another delivery coming through the back passage that she would have to be sign for. "Yes." She motioned to Lexie, one of the manicurists, mimicking a hurry call, and, pulling Tess along behind her, headed for the employees lounge.

Fortunately the room was empty. After long experience pouring coffee for patrons, Crystal found herself naturally pouring a cup for Tess. It gave her an extra second or two to study the woman, and wonder about why she had come. It seemed unlikely it was to place a wreath on the chair at Garth's station.

Tess wore a simple knit jumper over a white tee shirt with her shaggy blond hair loose. She wore no make-up and the leather sandals on her feet were shabby. It looked as if she hadn't been having an easy time since her divorce from Garth.

She sank down on the leatherette sofa. "Thanks for taking the time to talk to me," she said, nervously pulling a cigarette out of her purse. Crystal motioned that she couldn't light it, since Logan would have a fit if someone smoked in his salon. Several of the operators had resigned when he put that rule into effect, right before the remodeling job. One of them had been Tess, but maybe she had left just because of Garth.

Several of the operators still smoked, but they did it outside in the parking lot. Which brought to mind one of the niggling questions that Crystal had been pondering since the murder, why hadn't anyone been smoking in the back at the time of the murder? It seemed so unlikely that no one . . . She brought herself back to the present, since Tess was speaking.

"I want to know who did it," she said, barely audibly.

"So you can, like, thank that person?"

The puzzled look on Tess's face told her that she did not share the feeling that Rita had. "Uh, no."

Crystal didn't think Tess wanted the information so that she could practice some vigilante justice, so she just waited for her to go on.

"I just want to be sure it wasn't . . ." She stopped, blinking back a tear. "I tried to get here the day it happened, but there were so many people." She sighed. "I have to know . . ." Sitting up straighter, she said, "I know you are at the center of things around here, and I thought maybe you could find out."

Crystal drew in her breath sharply. "Who do you think . . . ?"

"Tom."

"You mean Tom Kacey? The man who owns the movie theaters?"

"Yes. I, we . . ."

"He's a very kind man," said Crystal. "He wouldn't have, like, done this."

"He hated Garth," said Tess.

"Did you ask him?"

"How could I? He'd hate me for thinking it, or if he did it, then . . ." Tears filled the bottoms of Tess's eyes. "I'm so afraid."

Crystal put her hand on Tess's shoulder. "I don't think anyone suspects him, but I, like, may know a way to find out, without, like, arousing any suspicion. Leave it to me."

The voice on the phone was becoming familiar. Over the past few days, Wally had spoken to Crystal, the white-faced receptionist, several times, but this was the first time that Crystal had been the one to call. Her voice had a kind of quaver today, in addition to the up-talk she occasionally used, as if everything she was saying was a question. And indeed, after only a few seconds, Wally realized that she was being pumped by Crystal.

To put a halt to the inquisition and gather her thoughts, Wally said, "Wait a minute. Why are you asking me what the police know and who they suspect? You're the one who is right there in the middle of the investigation."

"I know," lamented Crystal. "But they won't, like, tell me anything directly. I only know what I can guess based on what I see."

"And up until now you sounded confident about what you told me you saw. So what happened?"

"Nothing specific. I just had a visitor."

"Ah. And whoever it was wants you to reassure her, or him, that the police don't suspect her. Him. Whatever."

"Sort of. Look, I know I can, like, trust you not to broadcast this. I had a visit from Tess Barkley, Garth's last ex."

"Oh, I know her. She used to work in another salon I went to a few times. What did she want? Is she afraid the police suspect her?"

"No, she wasn't anywhere around here that day. The police already got a statement from her boss. She was worried about someone else."

"Tom Kacey, the movie theater owner?"

"How did you know about him?"

"I've seen them together. They seem like a happy couple. I have also seen him in a shouting match with Garth. His face can get virtually purple, you know."

"I've noticed that," Crystal said, somewhat breathlessly. "Have you heard of anyone saying he might be a suspect?"

"I can look into it," Wally offered. "Don't worry, I won't raise any suspicions."

"Great. You know where to reach me."

Chapter Nine

The doorbell rang while Wally was cutting up vegetables for a quick stir-fry at dinner time. Looking at her watch, she predicted that it was another delivery.

Niki Stetson, dressed in the brown UPS uniform, stood on her doorstep with a package. "This one is from pretty far away," she said, smiling. "And it's for the bride." She handed Wally the electronic clipboard and waited while Wally signed.

Handing the heavy object back to Niki, Wally looked at the return address on the package and smiled. "I think I know who sent this."

Both women looked up as Debbie's car pulled into the driveway. "I bet she'll want to see that right away," said Niki, as she turned to go back down the walk.

Wally heard Debbie coming through the back door, so she brought the package into the kitchen. "Did anything else come today?" was out of Debbie's mouth before she had even hugged Wally.

"Isn't this enough?" Wally handed her the package, which she tore open immediately, revealing a beautiful jewelry box crafted of exotic koa wood.

"It's from Louise," said Debbie, reading the card. "Look, she sent it from Hawaii. Wasn't that sweet?"

Tears stung Wally's eyes. Louise was the one person she could have talked to about how she was feeling between the tension of the upcoming wedding and people wanting her to help with their lives and the murder investigation. Within seconds, if past occurrences were any indication, Louise would have had her out on a tennis court, running around, laughing and feeling better.

"Are you okay, Mom?"

"I'm alright. Sorry, I guess I'm just emotional about my little girl getting married."

"You've done this once already," Debbie reminded her.

Wally couldn't explain. All she could do was hug her daughter, very tight.

The ringing phone interrupted Elliot's thoughts. "My mother has a question," said Debbie, after a warm, loving greeting. "Please just answer it so she can get on with the important things she has to do. Then you and I can talk."

A mental image of his future mother-in-law with her ever present wedding notebook, checking off another detail, jumped into his mind. She seemed to have more energy than two people. "What is it?" he asked, after Mrs., er Wally . . . Mom got on the phone.

"I need to know if you have any suspicions about any of the other businessmen in town."

It took a second to realize that she was wearing her detective hat. That was okay. She was one sharp lady, and at this point, he could use the help. "Are you talking about the murder? Are you worried about Mr. uh, Nate?"

She chuckled, which she seemed to do every time he was in the awkward position of having to refer to one of Debbie's parents. "Of course not." Switching to a serious tone, she continued. "I can't say anything else about why, but I just have to reassure one person."

"You're asking a lot."

"I know. Can you help?"

"I can tell you that none of the business people outside of the salon are suspects. We haven't eliminated Logan."

"You're positive?"

"Do you want to be specific?"

"I really shouldn't. But you have been open with me, and I guess I should do the same. Someone was worried about the theater owner."

The suggestion that Tom Kacey had anything to do with the murder surprised Elliot, but he answered Wally honestly. "He was in Newark that day. We have confirmation."

"Oh. Well, good. I guess some people should learn to communicate openly, and then I wouldn't get dragged into these things."

As he hung up the phone, Elliot knew he should get back to work. Yet he looked at Debbie's picture on his desk for a long time. He could hardly wait to marry her, but he had to solve the case first.

Crystal put down the telephone receiver and sighed. That was the fifth time she had tried to call Tess. Where was she? Had she stopped worrying about her boyfriend, or was she out getting herself into trouble? Crystal knew Tess really needed to hear what Wally Morris had learned. It had been awfully kind of her to go to the trouble. She was quite a contrast from Crystal's own mother, who wouldn't go to the trouble to tear herself away from the television long enough to make dinner for her kids, let alone help someone out. And even though her mother was at least ten years younger than Mrs. Morris, she looked a heck of a lot older.

She dialed again, but Tess still wasn't home to get the call, and oddly, there was no answering machine.

There was little time to think about it, however, because the salon was jumping this afternoon. Logan himself was cutting hair for people who didn't have standing appointments, or the next best thing, a well known name, something he swore he'd never do. As usual he did it, as almost everything else, arrogantly.

The new trainee, Ilke, hovered next to Logan as he worked. Crystal knew, however, from reading Ilke's resume when she knew Logan wouldn't catch her, Ilke was an experienced hairdresser. Yet Logan required everyone who worked for him to go through a period of subservient labor while he filled their psyches with tales of his greatness.

"It is essential to consider the growth of the hair," he said, gesturing with his hand along the side of his client's head. "You cannot fight it, no matter how sharp your scissors. But you can coax it." He waved his comb with a flourish and smiled at himself in the mirror. Ilke turned her head to cough, as if a wave of the permanent solution being used at the next station was bothering her. For just a second Crystal thought she saw Ilke roll her eyes.

Logan had her hold a section of hair for him while he cut another section underneath. "I do not use clips in creating my styles, nor do I allow them anywhere in the salon." Crystal was familiar with that practice; it was a trademark of sorts, even though there seemed to be no benefit and made life difficult for the operators who did not have the luxury of slave labor.

"Hold it a little higher," Logan growled. "I cannot see under here."

The person in the chair, Mrs. Hardy, squirmed as her hair was twisted. Logan shot a look of fire at Ilke. She shrugged, a sure sign to Crystal that the 'vacation' she was on from her regular salon would not become permanent. The whole experiment of switching to a more prestigious salon would be chalked up to experience, and not a pleasant one at that. It had happened with at least a dozen other hairdressers 'in training' over the past few years, and the process of training, from start to finish, was more unpleasant with each passing year.

But Ilke would be one of the quickest to recognize that Logan's salon was not for her. It was not because she was a genius or anything, it was simply because Logan was the most obnoxious he'd ever been. Poor Mrs. Hardy, sitting innocently in his chair, might not be happy with the result of his efforts if he didn't get himself under control soon.

Crystal knew that Mrs. Hardy had been reluctant to let Logan cut her hair. She had been one of the people who swore by Garth, and had taken several days to decide to let someone else cut her hair. She had one of those really short cuts that require trimming every three weeks, which had helped tip the decision, since she had been due for a trim the very day of the murder and her hair was now positively shaggy.

Somehow, by the time the haircut was over, Ilke had vanished but Mrs. Hardy looked great. In fact, she looked better than when Garth cut her hair. An astonished look replaced the frown she'd worn, and she practically floated over to the reception desk with her credit card in her hand.

"I can't get over this," she said. "He's really better than . . ." she dropped her voice to a whisper, "Garth. I would never have guessed."

Crystal spent the time that the credit card took to be approved after she swiped it through the machine to study the new hairdo. She couldn't quite figure out how it was different from the way Garth did it, other than to say that somehow it seemed to flow better, as if Logan really did go along with the way Mrs. Hardy's hair grew, instead of fighting it and beating it, with a lot of gel and mousse, into submission. The hair was practically product free, bouncy, shiny and fresh looking, a definite improvement.

The salesman for the hair products would not be happy. Hopefully, since he had just been in on the morning of the murder, he wouldn't walk in right now and see that Logan was undermining his sales.

Crystal thought about that for a second. She wasn't sure she had told that nice police detective, Ryan, that the salesman had been there, since so many people had come in that morning. She made a mental note to tell him. Hopefully Ryan, and not his partner, that Detective Scott person, would come in soon. Ryan was really cute, although so shy. It took everything she had to get him to have a conversation, even about the murder.

Maybe she should try to convince him to let her have a copy of the list, just in case she remembered something else and couldn't remember if she'd mentioned that person. It might mean that she'd have fewer reasons to call him but it would be a good idea, so that she wouldn't sound like an air head. Maybe she could even convince him to sit with her while she went through the list.

The phone rang again. It was time to get back to work.

Chapter Ten

"Are you sure you can handle this?" Wally asked Tillie as she helped her put on her rain hat.

Tillie's eyes, a somewhat faded version of the blue-green color of her son Nate's, sparkled. "Absolutely!"

A late spring rain was drenching the east coast, yet Tillie insisted on keeping the dress fitting appointment. Though she would have to wear a raincoat and wrap her cast leg in a garbage bag, it did not appear to dampen her spirits.

Wally opened the apartment door and carefully guided Tillie into the hall. There was a rail along one side of the corridor, interrupted only by the doorways of the even numbered apartments, and Tillie hung onto it, gingerly stepping on her broken foot as little as possible. Although the orthopedist had assured her that it was nearly healed, she still favored it. She smiled bravely during the long walk to the elevator, in the face of her nervousness about reinjuring herself.

The fall had eaten into Tillie's self confidence, Wally realized, watching the way she hesitated. Hopefully she would regain it with time.

A lady using a walker came toward them. She moved along slowly, occasionally straightening it out as it went sideways, Wally supposed, because one side of her body was weaker than the other. The front of the walker had wheels and the back had bright green tennis balls covering what Wally knew were very small slides. Many of the walkers in the building were similarly outfitted. Supposedly it made them easier to glide along on the floors, but Wally thought it also made them look sporty.

"How are you Tillie?" asked the woman, whose name, if Wally remembered correctly, was Frannie. She turned her attention to Wally. "We all still feel so terrible about the accident. It would never have happened if people listened to me. You can't put that kind of detergent in a washing machine." She paused, but not long enough. "Your mother-in-law was so brave. She's such a lovely lady, I just adore her. Where are you going?"

Tillie smiled. "To try on my dress."

"Oh, for the wedding? I'm sure it will look wonderful." She put out her hand to touch Tillie's arm. "But the weather is very bad."

Tillie patted her garbage bag wrapped leg. "I'll be okay. Wally will bring the car right up to the ramp."

"You are so sweet," said Frannie, looking at Wally. "You are so good to your mother-in-law. Some of the girls have daughters who just don't have time for them, but you . . ."

As her voice trailed off Tillie said, "I never had a daughter, but Wally is as wonderful as the best daughter could be."

Wally fought the urge she had to tear up, or to hug Tillie, which might knock her off her precarious balance. She decided that biting her lip was the best course of action.

Tillie wasn't finished though. "Nate is the best son, so he deserves such a wonderful woman."

"Sons? Ha," said Frannie. "They're even worse than some of the daughters."

Wally was truly uncomfortable now. Her own husband was an exception, it seemed, but she disliked what sounded suspiciously like it was about to escalate into a diatribe about either Frannie's own children or some other unfortunate resident of the building.

Her fears were confirmed when Frannie continued. "Poor Belle. Her son never comes to see her."

"We really have to hurry," said Tillie, cutting the woman

short and reaching for the elevator button. "I want to try that dress on."

Wally nodded. "It was good seeing you," she told Frannie, as the elevator doors opened.

Tillie didn't say anything again until the elevator doors had closed. "Poor Belle," she mimicked. "Her son visits every other day, but Belle is so forgetful she doesn't remember. Frannie believes her, but then, she's very gullible."

The dynamics of the people and personalities in Tillie's building always intrigued Wally. It also frightened her, making her respect all the more the way Tillie had adapted. She remained silent during the ride down to the first floor.

The lobby was full of people, more so than usual. It turned out that the mailman was late and the people were all waiting for the mail, the high point of some of their days. But since so many of them were hard of hearing, there was a lot of noise as each of them voiced their own opinion of why the mail was late. They not only voiced their opinions, they repeated them, as each tried to make his or her own point about the reason, and each ignored what the other was saying. It was almost comical. Wally heard snippets of conjecture.

"It's the rain," said a lady, scowling at the sky outside the glass doors. "They always say they go out in the rain, but I don't think so."

"Whether rain, sleet, snow or dark of night," quoted one sonorously toned old gentleman.

"It must be his day off," said someone else. "The mail always comes late on his day off."

"It was his day off yesterday. How many days off do you think he gets?"

"It's better if it's his day off. When the sub is on, she doesn't crush my Reader's Digest."

"How do you crush a Reader's Digest?"

"Oh, you know what I mean."

One woman approached Wally as she helped Tillie walk through the crowd. "Miriam! Where have you been? Your mother has been waiting."

Wally stopped, unsure of what to say. The woman was looking right at her, but was obviously confused.

"That isn't Miriam," said a man standing next to her. "There is no Miriam. She was the daughter of the lady who lived next door to you in Brooklyn."

"That isn't Miriam?"

"No." The man turned to Wally. "My sister gets mixed-up. Miriam died in seventy-five."

Finally they had made their way to the door. "Stay right here while I get the car," said Wally. Then, putting up her umbrella, she ran for it.

The ride over to the dress place was far less eventful than the trip from Tillie's apartment to the front door. An added bonus was that Penny, the saleswoman who had helped select the dress, was standing at the curb and helped get Tillie into the store. That was one of the best things about that dress shop; they did everything for the customer and never treated Wally, in her current role as Tillie's helper, like hired help the way some of the other places did. The orthopedist's office sprang to mind in that regard. They always expected Wally to get Tillie ready for the checkup on her foot, as if Wally were a nurse's aide.

Penny talked all the way into the store and into the back where the fitting rooms were. She told Wally to sit in a chair while she got Tillie ready, and although there wasn't coffee available due to the fear of stains on the merchandise, she made sure she was comfortable with a magazine before they went into the fitting room.

Elliot hoped that Wally would be back soon. Beside the problem he was having trying to get comfortable with what he was supposed to call her, he was now in the middle of what was practically a shouting match among the residents of Tillie Morris's apartment building.

She lived in a retirement building in the center of Grosvenor, New Jersey, not far from where Wally and Nate lived. Although she sometimes told stories about the strange things done by some of the women, who comprised the large majority of the building, Debbie's father was pleased to say that his mother never complained about giving up her house and moving there. She found companionship, entertainment and convenience in that building, and lately, with her broken leg, people to help out when they could.

Apparently, her story telling worked both ways. These people all seemed to know who he was and all about his wedding plans.

"You are marrying into such a wonderful family," said one of the residents, a tiny woman with bluish hair and dark penetrating eyes. "Tillie is such a lovely woman. I know her quite well, you know. We're very close. Her son, Nathan, and his lovely wife, Voltairine, take such good care of her."

Elliot stifled a smile. He knew that Wally never went by the name Voltairine, except on legal documents. She'd had to use it when she testified in court on a murder case a year earlier, and the coverage was extensive, so her real name had been much used by the local news media. Since this woman didn't know that Wally much preferred her nickname, Elliot concluded that she was not as close to Tillie as she wanted him to believe. He wondered why she felt it necessary to tell him that she was.

She paused, gazing around. "Not that Tillie usually needs such care, unlike some of these people. I hope her leg is all healed by the time of your wedding."

Another woman shook her head. "He has more to worry about than whether Tillie's leg is healed. He has to worry about solving the murder case so he can get some time off to get married."

"Oh, they'll let him off," said the first woman. "They wouldn't be so heartless."

Elliot reflected that this woman should have seen his boss that very morning. Marshall had made it clear, in no uncertain terms, that it was unlikely that anyone would get a minute off if the case wasn't solved. His exact words, delivered in a menacing manner, were: "If you think that I care about your wedding when my reputation is on the line yet again because of your stupid town, then you have another think due."

Elliot had to get this questioning done, even though both Mrs. Morrises weren't there to run interference for him. They had both warned him that these women would talk his ear off, and all around the subject, before he got any answers. Wally had further cautioned him that many of the residents were several cards short of a full deck.

He really only needed to talk to three of them, those who had been in the salon that morning. But two others had come to him when they heard he was coming, to tell him that they had been out in town that morning and were sure they had important information for him.

"Okay, ladies," said Elliot. "If we could get started. I'd like to ask that the three women who were in the salon each talk to me separately, so that we don't get each others' observations mixed up."

"Good luck, young fella," said a man who reminded him of his grandfather. "They've been talking about it for days, all together." He turned to the women. "Vivian, Esther, and Gertie go sit there."

The tiny blue-haired woman, who turned out to be Esther, bristled. "Who put you in charge?" But she went over to the indicated chair. Vivian, a much taller but obviously arthritic woman, told Gertie, a myopic, nervous looking octogenarian to go over to the chair, and after explaining it loudly she followed, slowly.

The man shrugged and herded everyone else out of the room, then came back to stand guard and keep the others out.

Elliot cleared his throat as he opened his notebook. "I'll need your full name."

Vivian looked at Esther. "Just like that other one."

Elliot did not need to be reminded that he was following behind the work that the Grosvenor P.D. in the guise of Dominique and the County Sheriff's Department, with Davis in charge, had done. He only hoped that the skimpy information they had provided, which he had already reviewed, would be enhanced by his questions.

But the women had little additional information, if any. They were all there having their hair done, one by Logan, as she proudly stated as if that were a badge of distinction, and they were all under the dryers at the time of the actual murder. Esther was sure that she heard a lot of shouting, but Vivian assured Elliot that not only was Esther somewhat deaf under the dryer, she was also sound asleep.

Gertie was fairly quiet during the discussion. It seemed to Elliot that she wasn't really listening. "They really should do something about all those people," she said, half to herself. "It's like Grand Central Station in there."

"What do you mean?"

"Well, all those deliveries. Can't they confine them to the back area? Why do they have to all walk around where I'm trying to relax?"

"You go to the beauty parlor to relax?" asked Vivian. "I thought you did enough relaxing here."

Gertie made a face, something that Elliot supposed was outrage, but on her looked more like a prune sadly sucking lemons. "What is that supposed to mean?" she said. "Are you saying that I'm lazy?"

"We gave you one job, not so big, and you didn't even do that right."

"Ladies," said the old man. "You shouldn't be arguing. This poor boy is depending on you to help him so that he can solve the case and get married."

"He should ask his future mother-in-law for help," said Vivian. "She's the one who solved those other cases."

Regardless of his annoyance at their assumption that he didn't have anything to do with solving the other cases, and his guilt that it was at least partially true, Elliot wished that Mrs.—Wally would show up and help him, if not with the investigation, at least with these women. He also needed the spectators to stop commenting from the doorway, so he closed the door before he started a fresh page in his notebook.

The next question was directed to Gertie. "Can you tell me who you saw walking around?"

She seemed reluctant to speak. Elliot thought he saw tears in her eyes and she sat hunched, turned away from Vivian and her insults. "A man came with a water jug," she said hesitantly. "It was bigger than my great grandson. Another man . . ."

"I saw him," Vivian interrupted. "His pants were so low that when he bent down you could see the crack in his tuchas."

Gertie glared at the woman. "Yes, well, he came and did something to the wall."

"That was an air conditioning repair man," said Vivian.

"The air conditioning wasn't even working that day," said Gertie in disbelief. "It was so hot in there."

Vivian slapped her knee in disgust. "That's why he was there."

Elliot tried to bring the conversation under control. "Please, Ma'am. Who else did you see?"

"I saw the UPS person, and someone in a FEDEX suit. Why can't they combine so just one man delivers?"

"How stupid!" said Vivian. "Maybe they should just tell all the people who want to send them things that they have to bring it to a central location."

"What's your problem?" said Gertie.

"You are taking too long. There was also a man to fix one of the hair dryers, a mailman, someone from the bakery came with bagels, although that boy with all the jewelry never brought me one, he just disappeared."

"Do you mean Dakota?" Elliot asked. Dominique's report on him had said that he was somewhat clueless when she talked to him but that Wally had seen him just before the bump and didn't think there would have been time for him to go into the consultation room.

"Yes."

"He brought me a bagel," said Esther. "I wondered why."

"But you didn't say anything? That was my bagel!"

"I'll get you another one."

Esther's sarcastic tone was not wasted on Vivian, who glared at her before resuming her statement. "There was a woman who came to deliver coffee . . ." Vivian's voice trailed off. Elliot hoped that she had just remembered something important.

But all she said was, "I don't understand why they can't just serve normal everyday coffee? None of this Vietnamese cinnamon vanilla for me."

Esther perked up. "That's Viennese."

Elliot wrote everything down, with the sinking feeling that this information would be of little use.

He cleared his throat. "Ma'am? Is there anything you can add to the statements?"

Esther looked at Gertie as if she were beneath contempt, leaving Elliot to wonder why the woman had that reaction. But she shook her head.

Stealing a glance at his watch, Elliot wondered how long a dress fitting took.

In less time than it took for Wally to determine from the magazines what the latest lipstick shades were for the season, Penny was back, helping Tillie take her place in front of the mirror. Scowling a bit, she reached down the front of the dress and rearranged Tillie's breasts, getting them lined up better. "There, that does it. Just look. Beautiful, no?"

When she got over her shock at the woman's familiarity, Wally had to admit that the dress came out even better than she had first thought. The color was beautiful, and it fit Tillie quite well. If only they could be sure that the Air Cast would be a thing of the past before the wedding, everything would be perfect. If not, little Jody the flower girl would be assigned to stand in front of that leg in all the pictures.

Tillie studied herself in the mirror, turning carefully to see the back. "It does look pretty, doesn't it?"

Penny, who was looking at herself in the mirror more than at Tillie, smiled broadly. "Gorgeous. Especially with your beautiful hair."

Tillie demurred, "Oh, it hasn't been done in over a week. But I did have a perm, so it's staying in better."

"Just beautiful," said Penny.

"Can we take it home?" asked Wally.

"I suppose. But remember, if you want to check it again when you can wear regular heels, I'm here."

Wally waited as they took the dress off and bagged it for Tillie, then loaded it into her car while Tillie brandished her credit card. With any luck, Wally thought, she could get Tillie back to her apartment and herself home in time to make dinner. A quiet dinner would really be wonderful after the afternoon she'd just had.

She could tell, though, the minute she walked Tillie back into her building, that she wasn't quite done for the day. A loud argument emanated from the dining/meeting room, and several people crowded around the door.

"What's going on?" Tillie asked.

"Those old biddies . . ." said one woman.

"Who are you to call someone else old?" asked another woman.

"I'm younger than you."

Wally coughed loudly. Everyone turned to her, and she smiled. "Sorry, I had something caught in my throat."

"You'd better take care of that," said a woman. "My sister had that, and she needed throat surgery. The next thing you know, you have a voice box that sounds like a machine when you talk."

Tillie hobbled over to the door of the dining room. "Is Elliot in there? We were supposed to meet him here."

"Yes," said the old man. "You are just in time to save him, unless it's too late."

Wally studied his eyes and saw humor. It was refreshing after the serious way that everyone else debated every little thing. She knocked on the door, and waited, peering through the glass window.

Elliot bounded to the door, and pulled it open quickly. A broad smile greeted Wally and Tillie as he ushered them into the room.

"How was your fitting?" asked Esther. "Did you check the seams? Sometimes they are so careless nowadays."

"They should be perfect," Vivian piped in, "for what you paid."

Wally wondered how they knew how much the dress was. It didn't seem likely that Tillie would have told them. She knew better. Whatever it cost it would be too much or too little to some of the women in the building, and some might even wonder aloud whether Tillie should think her granddaughter was worth more than that.

Tillie, in confirmation of Wally's theory about keeping her own counsel, did not respond.

"Did you find out anything?" Wally asked, noting that Elliot's shoulders were stiff. He was gritting his teeth too, if Wally's guess was correct about the cause of the bulges on each of his cheeks.

"The ladies have been very cooperative," said Elliot. He turned to them. "If you remember anything else, please call me."

Esther, Vivian and Gertie seemed somewhat miffed at being dismissed but Tillie mollified them by asking for help back to her apartment. After a short argument about who should walk on which side of her they left, practically finding themselves enveloped by the crowd in the hall waiting for the elevators.

It was nearly dinner time, and the staff had to set up the tables. From what Wally had heard, dinner was mostly a time for the residents to irritate the waitresses by changing their orders and ask for what each other had. With emotions heightened by the murder and investigation, it would only be worse. Wally, who had once spent an awful summer waiting tables in the Catskills, felt only sympathy for the kitchen staff.

Chapter Eleven

Logan was on a tear. Crystal knew enough to stay well out of her boss's way on days like this, and unfortunately there had been quite a few lately. He'd had a fit when the entrance to the salon was blocked by wires for the news crews that kept coming out to report on the progress the police were making. He'd actually yelled at reporter B. J. Waters for annoying his clients.

Another time, he had chastised one of the manicurists because she didn't bring an egg roll along with his hot and sour soup from the Chinese restaurant next door. He didn't care that the restaurant was out of them because of all the reporters in town. "Why do they always show up here at lunch time?" he'd shouted.

Crystal had tried to explain that they were there so they could be 'live' on the noon news. They were also there for the news shows at 5:00 and 6:00, as well as 11:00, when the salon was long closed for the evening and there seemed to be no reason to stand in front of it to do a report, but since that didn't affect Logan, he hadn't seemed to notice.

This morning's temper tantrum started soon after the mail delivery, but, although several bills had arrived, none of them seemed to be the cause of the eruption. Instead, Crystal was convinced it was the hand addressed greeting card that was the cause of the whole tirade, including the door slamming and foot stomping that Logan was now engaged in, to the amusement of a four-year-old who had accompanied his mother while she had her hair cut, color enhanced, and blown to look like the latest hot Hollywood style.

Crystal wondered about the card. It wasn't Logan's birthday, or the holiday season, during which hundreds of Christmas cards flowed in for the salon and its employees. It wasn't Father's Day, not that his ungrateful children would send a card to him at the salon. Besides, he wasn't reacting as if he enjoyed the contents of the envelope. In fact, he ripped up the card right after reading the inside. If he threw it away, Crystal didn't see any sign of it, including in the wastebasket in Logan's private office, which she snuck into after he grabbed his car keys and ran out the door.

One thing she found, however, was the envelope the card had come in. It had no return address, but Crystal noticed that it was postmarked Tewksbury, New Jersey. She vaguely knew where that was, but never knew anyone who came to the salon from there. If she had a minute later, she decided, she might look up the town on the computer and maybe match it with an address. Maybe she'd get a clue about her boss' bizarre behavior.

Eunice's puzzled expression told Crystal that her sleuthing in Logan's inner sanctum had not gone unnoticed. For a second Crystal stood, paralyzed, wondering what to do. Weighing what she knew about Eunice's natural sweetness, she opted for a strong, virtuous defense. She didn't think that Eunice would intentionally say anything to Logan, but she might, by accident, mention the foray into his office and that wouldn't do at all.

"I'm like, so worried about Logan," said Crystal.

The hairdresser, generally as nonjudgmental as they come, asked, "Why?"

"Didn't you see how upset he was? He got a note from someone and nearly went postal."

The only reaction she got to that statement was a slow blink of Eunice's long false eyelashes. Crystal had to continue.

"So, I'm like, I have to try to see who it came from, to help him if I could. You know how he is, always trying to be so strong, and I know he'd never ask for help." It occurred to Crystal that her babbling was getting her nowhere. Who was going to believe that a twenty-three-year-old receptionist could or would help her tyrannical boss?

Eunice cocked her head to one side, a tiny smile deepening the lines beside her mouth. "So what did you find out while you were snooping?"

Sweat popped out on Crystal's forehead at the same time that her extra-strength antiperspirant went off duty. "I, uh . . ."

"Don't worry. I won't say anything. But if you found something out, you should probably tell your honey."

"My *what?*"

"What's his name? Ryan? If you help him solve the murder, I'll bet he'd be grateful."

Suddenly Crystal felt weak in the knees.

As she turned to go, Eunice called back over her shoulder, "Don't worry so much. I may not be as dumb as you seem to think, but other people are." Then she smiled.

It was time for Crystal to take a break.

She really was lucky, she reflected as she went down the basement steps to the break room, that Eunice was not going to tell on her. Still, the uncomfortable clamminess she had experienced while worrying about it made her feel funny. She stopped outside the door to wipe her face with a tissue.

Voices from the other side of the wall, which Logan had not bothered to soundproof as well as he had the upstairs areas, drifted through the closed door. Crystal took her hand off the doorknob because the voices sounded angry.

"You have to give up," said one voice. Crystal wasn't sure who was speaking, but was even more curious who he was speaking to. Was it the murderer and did someone else know?

"I do not!"

Lexie! It was Lexie, one of the many salon employees, talking. Crystal held her breath.

"There is no way you can get away with it," said the first voice, which Crystal decided was Jordan. "Someone will tell the police."

"Do you need something?" said another voice behind Crystal.

With a gasp, she whirled around, ending up staring into the eyes of Armond. Now the second favorite hairdresser of the women, the short, pockmarked man with the receding hairline seemed to have suddenly grown taller. He certainly stood straighter and exhibited far more confidence since Garth's death. If anyone could be said to have benefited from the death of the other hairdresser, Armond, in many subtle ways, had.

Now this formerly mild, dweeby sort of non-man struck real fear into Crystal. "I, I, I . . . was just going into the break room."

"You, you, you," he said, not kindly, "were eavesdropping. Why don't we go in and see how our co-workers feel about that?" He reached for the doorknob and turned it, pushing the door open. Light from the interior flooded the dim hallway, causing Crystal's eyes to blink while they adjusted.

The two people in the room, little Lexie, the waxer and sometime manicurist, and Jordan, wearing a tight tee-shirt to display his newly flat, liposuctioned belly, broke away from staring at each other, but their anger still hung in the air.

Armond stepped between them. While he towered over Lexie, he was several inches shorter than Jordan, who advanced on him with clenched fists.

"Stay out of this," Jordan hissed. "It's none of your business."

Armond backed away, but only out of reach. "While Logan is not here, I have to make sure that nothing happens."

Jordan turned bland eyes toward him. "If you leave right now, nothing will."

"Are you threatening me?"

Crystal, having recovered sufficiently, and also realizing that her eavesdropping would go unchallenged, put up her hand. "Look. We all have to cooperate. Logan is, like, counting on us." She looked at each of the men. "Why don't you both go back upstairs? You each have an appointment due in, like, five minutes."

As the men shuffled past her, still keeping a distance from

each other, she stood between the door and Lexie. "I think we need to talk," she said.

Lexie sat down on the battered couch and pulled her legs up under her. Her head slumped forward letting her cloud of blue-black, color-enhanced hair fall over her face. When she looked up, she said, "I may be in trouble."

Crystal felt a wave of fear for her co-worker and wasn't sure she wanted to know what Lexie was about to say. At the same time, she felt a thrill of hearing something really juicy and was anxious for the girl to continue. "This is about Garth, isn't it?"

"Yes."

Crystal's stomach knotted and she struggled to keep her face neutral. "Tell me."

Tears spilled over onto the girl's cheeks, but she didn't wipe them away. Instead, she smiled, and gulped. "This is so silly for me to cry over. He is dead, after all, and he can't hurt me anymore."

Crystal pulled a tissue out of the pop-out box on the wicker end table and handed it to Lexie. She gratefully took it, wiped her eyes, and blew her nose. Then, ready, she explained.

"You probably don't know this, but Garth and I were . . ."

"I can, like, guess. I've seen the way you watched him."

"He was such a flirt. Anything female." She frowned. "I know it was only for business, at least most of the time."

Crystal remained silent, resisting the urge she had to thoroughly shake the stupid woman in front of her. Lexie was at least five years older than she, probably twenty-nine already, although she looked far younger, being so tiny and with her bright blue eyes partially obscured by the bangs of her inky hair. She was still capable, however, of believing in a man like Garth. Of course, many women had been taken in by him, but that didn't make Lexie seem any smarter.

"He told me that he loved only me. He even gave me a ring."

"He was going to marry you?"

"Yes."

This completely contradicted everything Crystal knew about

Garth. He never married anyone unless it was to his advantage, and what would be the advantage of a marriage to Lexie, who had no money? "Why haven't I seen the ring?"

"He asked me not to wear it in public. He felt that people might ask questions."

"And he thought that would be a problem?"

"Well, he thought that it might cut into his tips if some of those women knew he wasn't eligible anymore. I completely understood."

Because you're a complete fool, thought Crystal, as she shifted her body on the couch to get a better look at Lexie.

"Do you have some information that could help the police?" Crystal asked.

"Well, I . . . Maybe. Jordan told me that I have to tell the police, but I wanted to handle it on my own. He said to give up. I'd never be able to handle it."

"What?"

Lexie started to cry again. "You know that apartment building I live in? Well, my uncle sold it to me for a dollar. Garth had me sign it over to him when we got engaged, but no one knew that, and I was still the manager. Garth wanted to evict someone, well, actually everyone, but one person in particular because he wasn't paying the rent and his apartment is always a mess. Garth was so mad when I didn't do it."

"I don't understand this. Why did you give him the building?"

"I thought, well, when we got married, I would own the building with Garth, right? So what did it matter?"

"Did you sign anything?"

"Oh, yes. Garth got a form from the internet and filled it out. I signed and got it notarized. So did Garth."

Trying to make sense of what Lexie was saying, Crystal asked, "Why haven't you told anyone about this?"

"Because I'm afraid."

"Of what?"

"Well, I found out, just before he was murdered, that Garth was lying to me. He wanted the apartment building more than he wanted me."

While this did not come as a surprise to Crystal, she had no desire to hurt Lexie. "Oh?" was all she could think of to say that would be nonjudgmental.

"So if I tell, I'll probably get thrown out. Garth was planning to go condo. I can't afford it."

It was all clear to Crystal, who realized that sooner or later Lexie would be out on the street. It didn't seem to have occurred to her yet, but another problem had.

Crystal handed Lexie another tissue. "You're afraid that if the police knew that you found out that Garth wasn't going to actually marry you, but just wanted the building, they'd, like, think you had a motive."

Lexie stood up and turned away. "You know, I guess I did. I wasn't sure until now, but he was just using me."

No duh, Crystal bit back, bruising her lips in the process. "Can I ask you something?"

The waxer turned back to face Crystal. "If you're asking whether or not I killed Garth, I promise I didn't. I was in the middle of a major total body hair removal."

"But," said Crystal, as delicately as she could, "those are done behind closed doors, just a few steps down from Room A, and you have to go in and out during the waxing."

Lexie's blank expression was soon replaced by understanding and then despair. "I swear I didn't do it! You've got to help me!"

"I'll see what I can do."

Wally watched as her next door neighbor Tabitha struggled her little three-year-old-legs up the ladder and swung them over to the top of the slide. Grasping both sides of it carefully, she looked around the yard for her mother. Marla smiled up at her, and waved.

The two women had been discussing the plans for the wedding, Debbie's tendency to make last minute changes and Wally's reluctant involvement in the murder investigation. Marla had asked several questions that Wally couldn't answer and their conversation had broken off in an awkward silence.

"Here I go, Mommy," said Tabitha. Pushing off, she leaned

back and lifted her feet so that her sneakers wouldn't slow her down. "Wheeeee!"

"She seems to be doing well," said Wally, from her side of the fence, glad there was another topic they could discuss.

Marla nodded, and almost instantly, tears formed in her eyes. "I feel so lucky. A year ago we thought she was deaf. Now she speaks almost as well as the other kids."

Tabitha came over to her mother's side. "Can I go again, Mom?"

"Yes, sweetheart." She watched her daughter climb the ladder. "I can't believe the difference."

"It's astonishing."

"I still feel bad that I didn't know what was wrong. If I had I would have stopped giving her dairy products sooner."

"Well," said Wally, "how could you know? It never affected the other children, did it?"

"No. But I should have known. Or at least the pediatrician should have."

"Don't berate yourself about it. Just be glad you found out and could correct the problem."

"But it was such a waste," said Marla, never taking her eyes off Tabitha, "everything I did before that. We had actually had Tabitha fitted for hearing aids, when her whole problem was her head was filled with so much fluid that she couldn't hear."

Although she could see the pain on her neighbor's face, Wally knew there was nothing to be gained by her guilt. "You have to let it go."

"I know. It doesn't help Tabitha, but I feel stupid."

"Look at it this way. You figured it out."

"But that's just it. I didn't figure it out. A stranger had to tell me."

This was news to Wally, who had watched Marla's anguish as she dealt with Tabitha's problem. "What do you mean?"

"I was really upset one day and mentioned it. Instead of just telling me she was sorry, the woman asked me if I had ruled out a lactose-based problem."

"How on earth did she know about that?"

"Oh, she explained that her brother had it. His parents thought he was deaf for seven years until he got pneumonia. They were told to cut out milk products because of a medication he was given and also because of the phlegm factor," she paused, making a face at the thought, "and they didn't reintroduce the milk products until several weeks after he was well. When they started him on milk again he cried because he couldn't hear anymore. That was when they realized he was hearing, and that his speech had really cleared up. So they took him off milk again, and bingo, he could hear perfectly." She looked at Tabitha, who was climbing the ladder again. "Just like her."

Tabitha was tiring. She came over to her mother and put up her arms. Marla bent down and picked her up, cradling her head against her shoulder. The little girl was taking extra long blinks and seemed to rest. As the two of them waved goodbye and went into the house to take a nap, Wally wished she could take one, too.

Chapter Twelve

Wally hurried down Grove Street—the central street in Grosvenor—and in her rush barely noticed one of her friends on the opposite sidewalk. She had to get to the post office before 12:30 to mail the check to the band, which she was supposed to have had in their hands by yesterday. Instead, she had mistakenly sent a check to the florist two weeks earlier than their deadline. Telling no one about her error, particularly not Debbie, she'd called the band leader and explained, but not feeling that this was a good time to take chances on people's benevolence, she felt she had to hurry. It wasn't that the details for the wedding were getting to her, she really had everything organized, but her mind was wandering, particularly as the school year wound down. All those end-of-year projects, especially the presents for the dads and granddads, had to be finished. Wally felt as if her hands were permanently covered with glue.

The post office was rarely crowded on a normal day and she was finished a few minutes later. She took her time walking back to her car, taking a few moments to relax in the spring sunshine. Suddenly a hand reached out from one of the doorways, and dragged her inside a store.

"What the—?"

"Shh."

Wally looked around. She found herself inside Resplendence Salon, with her hand still being held by Crystal. The girl looked alive for a change; underneath her white makeup her cheeks were flushed. Her dark eyes sparkled with some secret, animating her whole face despite the morbid lipstick she wore on her pursed lips. She still held her index finger up, with her nearly black fingernail touching her mouth in the international sign of 'shush.'

"There is something you have to hear," Crystal whispered, bending her spiky, coifed head close to Wally. Then in a loud voice, she said, "Good afternoon, Mrs. Morris. Are you here to have your nails done?"

That was just about the last thing on Wally's mind, but the look in Crystal's eyes convinced her to play along. "Y-yes," she stammered. Regaining her equilibrium, she stood a little taller and spoke a little louder. "I am. They are a wreck."

"Lexie is the only one free," said Crystal as she led the way to the girl's chair. "But she'll do a beautiful job."

Wally watched as the girl jumped at hearing her name. Her eyes were rimmed red, and her nose was almost the same shade. That she had been crying didn't take a lot of detective work, but the reason behind it might.

Wondering what she had gotten herself into, Wally sat down. Her stomach growled, but considering the situation, she knew that lunch would be late.

Crystal leaned down and whispered into Lexie's ear. She only moved away when Lexie began to assess Wally's nails while removing the vestiges of glue and the clear nail polish that she wore. Considering that the wedding loomed ahead, Wally had fought her usual urge to keep her nails very short, which was the standard for nursery school teachers who got involved in so many crafts. Yet she hadn't really bothered to shape them as they grew. She watched Lexie slip a rubber finger on to protect her own hands in preparation for several minutes of filing.

"Mrs. Morris's daughter is getting married soon," said Crystal. "So she wanted to, like, start getting her nails ready. Isn't that right, Mrs. Morris?"

"Uh, yes. I'm afraid I haven't been very good about it."

"Lexie will fix that, won't you?"

For her answer, Lexie sniffled some more. Wally worried that the manicurist would get an overdose of the permanent solution that was wafting through the air, what with all that sniffling. Her own eyes burned as she looked up at Crystal, who was gesturing, over Lexie's shoulder, with her head and eyes that Wally should try to get Lexie talking.

"Is something wrong?" Wally asked softly. Crystal smiled with satisfaction and walked away.

Lexie didn't speak until the receptionist was back at her desk. "Well, I . . ."

"Maybe I can help," Wally encouraged.

The look in the girl's eyes, what Wally could see of them through the fringe of long wispy bangs, was one of defeat. Lexie sighed, shifted position in her chair and spilled her guts. She talked about her relationship with Garth and the way he treated her, and included several horror stories, all while she worked on Wally's hands. Her story concluded just as the quick dry top coat was applied.

When she was finished, Wally went to sit in another chair to wait while her nails dried. She picked up a magazine, but the constant chatter around her was too distracting.

"Of course she loves him," said one woman wearing a full set of rollers to another. "Hello, she's got his name tattooed on her arm."

Wally tried harder to concentrate on the magazine. It had been a long-standing policy of hers to never read gossip magazines at any time but at the hair dresser or doctor's office. She wasn't having her hair done but she gave herself permission to indulge her secret interests in scandals and the like. Yet the voices kept intruding.

"I have to go to the train station this weekend to meet a lady. She's going to give me some Botox—cheap," said the second woman in rollers.

The first woman grabbed her arm. "Hello? Don't you listen to the news? Haven't you heard about these people who have liposuction and get all these problems? It's like having it done in a bodega—you get a quart of milk and some liposuction on your thighs. And you want to get Botox from some lady on a train?"

Wally wondered about both women. One who felt so free to dispense medical advice and state the obvious, and the other, who was the recipient of her attitude. But just maybe the first one had stopped the second one from making a big mistake. After all, little Tabitha had been the lucky recipient of some medical advice from a non-medical person.

After what seemed like forever, Lexie determined that Wally's nails were dry. "Thanks," Lexie said. "I feel better just talking about it."

Crystal was waiting for Wally when she got to the desk. "Tell me, is she, like, not one of the stupidest born-yesterday people you ever knew?"

Wally, not liking to speak ill of someone she'd just met, and actually not sure given the conversation she'd overheard, did not answer that question. "You wanted me to talk to her because you think she may help in the investigation, right?"

"Um, hm."

"Do you think she did it?"

"I don't see how. She is so small, and the police think there was a struggle first. Did you know about that?"

Wally grimaced. "That's because of the bumps I felt when I was leaning against the wall that day."

Crystal's eyes and mouth opened wide. "Ohhhhh. That explains it." She laughed. "I'm like, how did they know that? It figures it was you. Well, do you think we should tell the police about this? I kind of hate to, because Lexie told me in confidence."

"You want me to do it, don't you?"

"Boy, you really are a good detective." She smiled. "Enjoy your manicure."

Wally found herself on the street exactly forty-five minutes after she'd been plucked off it. The temperature had soared, perhaps only by contrast to the positively chilly salon, or perhaps due to the burden Wally now carried. She pondered that as she hurried back toward her car, glancing surreptitiously at her newly rosy nails. They did look quite pretty, and had cost her thirty dollars plus the tip, prices being what they were in Resplendence Spa and Salon. Instead of messing them up during lunch preparation, she opted for a quick trip to the deli. Stocking up on pickles and overstuffed sandwiches seemed like a wonderful idea to Wally, especially considering the likelihood that the ever-hungry Nate was starving.

He was already in the kitchen when she got home, and she could only see his back end since his front was deep inside the refrigerator, hunting for something to eat.

Wally stopped and showed him what she had brought home. He quickly switched gears, as well as dairy dishes for meat dishes and they had lunch on the table in no time.

"How is your sandwich?" Wally asked.

"Very good. It's really hitting the spot."

"I'm glad."

Nate took a sip of his iced tea and smiled. "Can I ask you something?"

"Uh, um, what?"

"What made you decide to have your nails done?"

"Oh, do you like them?"

"Yes. But why today?"

"I was, uh . . . It was kind of sudden."

Nate cocked his head to one side. "Oh?"

Wally chuckled. Maybe Nate should be investigating the case too. Not much got past him. "I got pulled into the Salon—literally."

"What is it this time?"

"One of the girls there had a relationship with Garth. He cheated her."

"Cheated on her?"

"No, well, maybe, probably, but that isn't what I meant. He cheated her."

"Who? How?"

"This girl, the one who did my nails. Crystal requested that I have them done."

Nate interrupted. "Crystal?"

"The receptionist."

For a moment Nate look puzzled. "She requested that you

get your nails done? Were they offending her? Who appointed her the nail police?"

Wally had to wipe her eyes, she was laughing so hard. "I'll never be able to explain if you keep this up." She slid her chair back, stood up, picked up the dirty dishes and went over to the sink. "Let me just tell you this before I'm an old lady."

"I promise to be quiet."

"Okay then. Lexie . . ." Nate started to open his mouth so Wally quickly explained, "the manicurist, at least part time, the rest of the time she's a waxer . . . as in hair removal, not auto body . . . this is tiring, could you just let me speak?"

"I haven't said a thing."

"Maybe not out loud, but you should see your face."

"Why? Has it changed since I shaved it this morning?"

"No." She poured some more iced tea for each of them and sat down. "Please."

Nate waved a go-ahead.

"Thank you. Lexie was apparently living with Garth in an apartment in a building that her uncle had owned but signed over to Lexie. Garth convinced her to give him the building when they became engaged, even though she couldn't tell anyone at the salon that they were engaged because Garth was afraid it would somehow cut into his income." Wally paused, weighing her next words. A few of the things she had heard since the investigation started had been truly disturbing and were about people she knew. "Now I am going to make a statement which you will just accept as fact and not question me about." She waited for a reaction. Nate merely blinked, but she took that as assent. "He befriended some of his lonely customers and capitalized on their generosity. Being single probably was really important for that to continue."

"Oh."

"Right. Anyway, Lexie came to understand, and this is important, *before* the murder, that Garth was just stringing her along. At least she had a partial understanding of that, in her own way."

"Not too bright, huh?" Nate concluded.

"No, and on top of that, she's pretty gullible."

"I see. And now you want to tell Elliot all about this. That's a relief."

Red flags went up in Wally's mind. "What's wrong?"

"Elliot needs some help or he is going to miss his wedding."

Wally frowned. "Yes, dear, I know that. Okay, I'll get right on it."

Every time Elliot felt as if he were making progress, he'd come up to a brick wall or dead end that eliminated a suspect.

Even though many people had alibis, this did not overshadow many people also having strong motives to want Garth Barkley dead. The list was lengthening each day and included everyone but the butcher, the baker, and the candlestick maker, although the owner of the Bagel Bay had not been a fan of either Garth or Logan. He had planned to expand his shop into the store that Logan acquired prior to the last renovation, but had been outmaneuvered, at least partly due to some bad information he received from Garth about the magnitude of Logan's sealed bid. Nevertheless, the Bagel Bay's owner had been eliminated as a suspect. Several witnesses verified that he was filling a big luncheon order the whole morning and had personally delivered it, at almost the exact time of the murder, thirty minutes away. Only his assistant cashier had been to the salon, to deliver more bagels.

The owner of Perfect Image Photography studio had also turned up. He was found hiding at his mother's house in Kearny, New Jersey. Unfortunately for him, he was found there by the irate mother of a Bar Mitzvah boy whose proofs were not delivered at the specified time. She would have killed him, or, at the very least, made him wish he were dead, if the local police hadn't intervened. Complaints against him and his studio had been filed with the prosecutors of both Essex and Morris counties as had claims against what was left of the business. Some of them, Elliot suspected, had even been made by people who had been involved with Garth, since any hard evidence linking them was now a pile of cinders. It seemed unlikely, however, that one of the people who had sued was either the one who set such a thorough fire to the building or the murderer, let alone both. Yet Elliot followed up on every person involved.

It was an eclectic group, headed, at least in intensity, by Abby Kent. She had filed an amendment to her original suit about the picture they had taken that ended up on the sides of buses without her permission even though the studio was now a pile of rubble.

The bulldozers had not demolished the remainder of the storefront until police and nearly every lawyer involved had a look at it. Nothing was left of the studio, or the fortune teller's room upstairs, but Elliot decided to stop there on his way to Tewksbury to see Ms. Kent. All he saw, however, was shredded police tape and rubble.

A woman in her late fifties standing near the corner caught his eye. She wore a flowered house dress and plastic mules, and her hair was in curlers. She had a little Pekingese dog with her on a retractable leash. She was not looking at the dog; instead she was staring at the debris of the building.

Elliot approached her, keeping his eyes on the dog. "What a cute little guy," he said to the woman.

She let out a puff of smoke from her cigarette. The plumes swirled around and back up her nose, as she said, "Girl."

"She's beautiful," said Elliot, smiling what Debbie called his charming grin. "Do you live around here?"

The woman became instantly wary. "Why do you want to know?"

"Oh," said Elliot. "I was just looking at this building here. Do you know what happened?"

"Are you a cop or a lawyer?"

"Both."

She appeared surprised, but laughed. "I guess with that double whammy I should talk to you about it." She waved her cigarette at the rubble. "Someone torched the place. I would think that's obvious."

"You mean on purpose?"

"It had to be. No one was here when it happened."

"How do you know that?"

"I saw the photographer leave. He was gone all day."

Elliot looked at the sign that had been on the door to the fortune teller. It said *Madame Celeste, One flight up*. "What about her?"

The woman stared at Elliot. "She wasn't here."

"How can you be sure?"

"Because she was in my kitchen, making lunch."

"You know her?"

The woman shook her head and grimaced as if she was tired of dealing with fools. "I am her."

A wave of embarrassment washed over Elliot. "Do you know anything about the fire?"

"I know I lost my business. Who is going to believe that Madame Celeste can tell the future if I didn't predict that fire and call the fire department before the building burned down?"

The tiny smile on her face told Elliot she had at least a small sense of humor. "I guess there was neither a fire alarm nor sprinklers, huh."

"That cheap landlord wouldn't put them in. I suppose it was because he was trying to get Claude and me out so he could sell the building like he wanted."

"Do you think he set the fire, this Mr. . . . what is his name?"

"Ted Donner. Nah. But I wouldn't be surprised if the fire didn't come as a shock to him." Elliot thanked her for the information. It was more to think about as he drove west.

It occurred to him that it was odd that Ms. Kent had gone all the way to Livingston to have her photo taken, yet had signed a sworn affidavit that she had never set foot in Grosvenor, let alone had her hair styled in the Resplendence Salon. Grosvenor was only minutes from Livingston, while Oldwick, in the center of the state, was almost an hour away. He speculated about it all the way west on 78 and then along the side roads.

It was a pretty area and Elliot enjoyed his ride. There was a kind of New England charm to the little town and Ms. Kent lived in one of the turn of the century homes along the main street.

She greeted him at the door with a frown. "My lawyer said

that I shouldn't talk to you. He thinks it might jeopardize my case."

Elliot studied the woman's pretty face, her raven hair and blue eyes, and decided that while she was not stupid, she could be easily influenced. He had no time, however, for another monkey wrench in the works.

"I am conducting a murder investigation, ma'am. You will have to answer my questions."

Ms. Kent gasped. "C-come inside. I'm sorry."

Elliot followed her into her house. There were few windows and the mature trees outside diffused what little light came into the living room, making it difficult to see. But Elliot could make out, with increasing clarity as his eyes adjusted, what he understood from his research to be some very good antiques. The Kents, both father and daughter, were well respected in the field.

Elliot sat on the love seat near the fire place, where Ms. Kent had indicated, and watched as she took her place on a chair opposite him.

"How can I help you?" she said. Her blue eyes were wide, scared, and she seemed to be taking very shallow breaths.

Notwithstanding Elliot's resolve to never let a pretty face influence his investigations, he decided to give her a break. He wanted open communication, and this up tight woman was likely to be anything but open if he didn't calm her down. "Please relax, Ms. Kent."

"Is it okay to call me Abby?"

"Yes. Abby. It would help our investigation if you explained your understanding of how your picture came to be on the buses."

"I never said that the picture could be used to advertise a beauty salon."

"Did you intend that it be used for anything other than personal photos?"

"I, um,"

"Ms. Kent?"

"Abby, remember? My lawyer won't like this."

"Why not?"

"He didn't want me to say that I had the pictures taken for another ad."

"Is that what happened?"

"Yes. Well, I guess you need to know this, because it explains about how I met Garth and ended up going to that studio. You see, it all started at an antique fair, actually a craft and vintage furniture market in the armory, but kind of upscale. It's hard to get in—you have to apply. The furniture must be of a certain quality, not just old, and the crafts are juried."

"Go on."

"You see, I deal in antiques. Like the ones here. I buy and sell them. And some of my pieces were in the armory."

"That's impressive. You have to know a lot about them to do that."

"Oh, I got the business from my father. He taught me most of it, although I took some courses in it too." She paused as if unsure how to proceed. "Someone I knew introduced me to Garth at the antique show. He was very charming, and he suggested that an ad with my photograph in some of the antiques publications, or even *New Jersey Monthly,* might be good for business. He suggested Perfect Image to take the picture, and said that he is a part owner and could get me a big discount, especially, he said, because I am pretty and not hard for the photographer to look at. He never said a word about Resplendence Salon or being a hair stylist."

"So you went to get a picture taken and it ended up being used to promote Garth's other business."

"Yes."

"And you sued because of that."

"Right. Wouldn't you? They had no right to do that."

"Did Garth lead you to believe he wanted anything other than to be a swell guy who got you a discount on a photograph you could use for advertising?"

Abby blushed a deep red. "You'd think I'd be old enough to know better."

"And did you use that picture for advertising for your business?"

"No. How could I? It wouldn't look authentic if the same picture used to sell a hair cut was being used to sell antiques. That's why I felt I had to sue."

"I see. Let me move off that subject for just a minute. You said in your deposition that you had never been to Grosvenor prior to those posters being put on the buses."

"That's true. I never set foot in the town, so I couldn't have been in the salon."

"Not that it matters, but never in your whole life?"

"I don't think so. It is such a small town, and there really isn't any reason I'd have to go there."

"There are several antiques shops there. You've never dealt with any of them?"

"I, um, I know that."

"So you might have been there?"

"Well, possibly. But definitely not in the last two years." She seemed very sincere.

"Okay, I'll accept that. But how about after the picture was taken?"

Abby's eyes clouded. "I have."

"On business?"

"Not exactly."

"Do you know anyone there?"

"I have a few friends who live near there. We went to a bar in town a few times. But I didn't have anything to do with the murder."

"Your alibi checked out," said Elliot, while studying Abby's face. He thought he detected something unsaid. "Is there something else?"

"I'm not dropping the suit. If he thinks I am, he is wrong."

"I don't think that Claude, the owner of Perfect Image, expects you to drop it. When I talked to him he seemed convinced that no one would drop any of the suits."

"I don't mean him."

"You can't mean Garth."

"No." She laughed. "Oh, I guess that was tacky. But it sounded weird. No, I meant Logan. He is going to have to pay."

"I assume you can prove damages," said Elliot.

"What? Oh, yeah, my lawyer mentioned that. He has it under control." She frowned. "I may have done something stupid though."

"Oh?"

"I sent a nasty letter to Logan. I hope it doesn't get me into trouble. It may have sounded threatening."

Elliot made a note to check it out. While he had the distinct feeling that Abby was being straight with him, he was not going to rely on that. He would have to be sure. And he wondered about something else too.

"You don't seem convinced," Abby said, staring at Elliot.

"What? Oh, I'm sorry. I just thought . . . Who did you say introduced you to Garth?"

Abby smiled. "I didn't." Suddenly her expression changed into a frown. "I can't remember who it was. There were a lot of people I knew at the show at the armory. Is it important?"

Standing, Elliot handed Abby his card. "I don't know. If you remember, or have anything else to tell me, please call."

She took it, and sighed. "I never asked to be involved in this."

As Elliot drove away, he wondered if anyone had asked to get embroiled in Garth Barkley's business. The man had brought his end upon himself, of that Elliot had no doubt.

Chapter Thirteen

Wally pushed the door open and practically ran into Resplendence Salon and Spa. Just getting out of the intense sunshine should have been enough to cool her off, but now that she was a woman with a mission, to solve the case in a hurry, she was running on high and perpetually warm. She stopped in front of the receptionist for a moment to let the delicious air conditioning settle over her.

The chalk white make-up on Crystal's face split at the dark red lips into a smile. "You didn't, like, have an appointment today, did you Mrs. Morris?"

At the sound of Wally's name, the person standing next to Crystal raised her own head. Wally saw that it was Dominique and knew with certainty that she had come to the right place, apparently at the right time. "You are both just who I am looking for."

Dominique smiled, her beautiful face neatly framed by her black hair. "Are you here to help?" asked Dominique.

"Is it okay if I pitch in?"

Dominique looked around, turning her head until she spotted Ryan talking to Logan. Wally followed her eyes, gauging that her voice could not be heard over the whir of the hairdryers. "I guess you don't want him to know, do you?"

"Well," said Dominique, "maybe we could keep this just

between us, at least for now. Crystal, is there someplace we could go to talk?"

"Let's go to the break room. We can talk down there."

Wally followed Dominique and Crystal to a doorway that she hadn't noticed before. Crystal opened it, and going through, Wally found herself standing at the top of a flight of wooden stairs leading down to the basement. The cinder block walls that lined the narrow passage way at the bottom of the steps were painted a soft green, as was the cement floor. The effect was of smooth sterility, but on closer inspection, as she walked along behind the younger women, she could see nicks in the paint on the walls and scratches on the floor.

The break room, too, on first glance, seemed bright under the fluorescent lights, and warm. But the furniture, when Wally sat down, was not only shabby, it was downright lumpy.

Wally apologized for being abrupt. "I'm working with very little time. Can we go over this?"

"Yes." Dominique handed her clipboard to Wally. "Here is a list of all the people Crystal remembers seeing that morning. The next page has a list of additional people seen by other witnesses. The third page is a list of people we haven't been able to prove were not in the salon even though they say they weren't. Since the sources for those people being placed at the scene are shaky, as in some of the people in the retirement building, we haven't put a real push on establishing firm alibis."

Wally took the pages and went over them thoughtfully. "Very good," she said, when she had finished the first. "I think that's everyone I saw." Turning to the second, she read about halfway down and started laughing. "I think there's been a widespread case of imaginitis here." She held the page up to Dominique.

"Why do you say that?"

"Look here. It says Dr. Fisch."

"Yes."

"Well, see, that's the problem. A) He isn't a doctor; he is a pharmacist. B) He wasn't here that day. He's been in Hawaii with Louise for weeks."

Dominique inspected the list more closely. "The witness who says she saw him was one of the people in the retirement building. She remembers he smiled back at her."

"Oh," said Wally. "He loves those people, at least according to Louise. They are among his favorite customers. He flirts with them unmercifully."

Crystal looked puzzled. "Really?"

Dominique nodded. "That would explain why he hasn't returned my phone call. I left a message on his machine. We felt we had to check it out since the pharmacy is so close to the salon."

"Didn't they tell you at the store that he was away?"

"Ryan was supposed to go over there. I don't know if he went."

Crystal squirmed on her seat. "I'm sure he will."

The vibration of a budding romance wafted over to Wally. How nice, she thought as she turned back to the list. Maybe something good would come out of this mess.

There were even more delivery people listed than she remembered. She hadn't noticed the bagels being delivered, which Crystal had listed on her page, and she hadn't noticed the UPS delivery which Crystal didn't have on her list. She reasoned it may have come during one of the times Crystal was away from her desk and may not have been one that required a signature. It did strike her as odd that the delivery came in the early afternoon, since hers always arrived after four, but even though it was only a few blocks away, there was no way to predict that the times would be at all similar. The people who lived around the corner from her got their mail two hours earlier, except on days that the sub was on, so maybe the UPS deliveries were made at varying times of day depending on which driver's route the salon was on.

A person handing out leaflets was listed on the page. That struck Wally as odd, particularly since a NO SOLICITING notice was posted prominently on the front door. She put her finger on the entry and raised a questioning eyebrow.

"We wondered about that, too," said Dominique. "I haven't been able to figure out what it means. The lady who said she got a leaflet can't find it and no one else remembers it happening."

"Who was that?"

"Gertie Irving."

"Oh, I see. She's often confused." Wally noticed that the UPS delivery that she hadn't seen was also reported by Gertie, as was the sighting of Dr. Fisch. In all likelihood she was, to be kind, mistaken.

"That would explain it," said Crystal. "I'm like, I don't think one of those solicitors ever snuck past me." She glanced at her watch. "I have to get back to the desk. You can stay down here if you want, although it's about to get pretty crowded. Three people signed up for lunch right about now."

"We'll go up then," said Dominique. "I have to get back to Ryan, and make sure he's following up on these leads."

"I have to go too," said Wally. She stood up and walked to the door. "I'll think about the list." What she really wanted to do was check with Tillie and a few other people she knew who were in town.

They had to step aside to let Lexie and another manicurist get into the break room, and Wally had to walk back down three steps from the top of the staircase so that Crystal could open the door, which opened inward, toward the stairs. She noticed that Crystal looked out into the salon before going through the door, as if being careful not to collide with someone walking past the door.

"Do you think," said Wally, "that someone could have hidden in that stairway?"

"You mean the murderer?" asked Dominique.

"Yes."

Dominique considered the idea. "I suppose. That would explain how he or she got around without anyone seeing anything. The murderer could have just waited until the hallway was clear. It's something to consider."

Wally was deep in thought as she went back home. There were a lot of things to consider.

* * *

Elliot gritted his teeth and pushed the door of the pharmacy open. He was annoyed not only with the new detective that Dominique was partnered with but also with himself for being so distracted that he was actually wasting his own time.

If she'd said it once, she'd said it six times. Not that his future mother-in-law repeated herself, it was more that she was really upset about her friend Louise being away. Elliot, to be truthful, was kind of happy about it, since he felt he had somewhat more privacy without Wally's best friend around pumping everyone for information about wedding gifts, honeymoon plans, and even sleeping arrangements. Since Debbie didn't keep much from her mother, he believed that Louise, whom he privately called Lousy in moments of frustration, was in the busybody business for herself.

It had been so quiet lately and Elliot was enjoying it so much, that when the subject of Norman Fisch possibly being in the salon on the morning of the murder came up, he hadn't noticed. That was why he was so aggravated with himself. He could have immediately responded that the man couldn't possibly have been in the salon and that anyone who thought he was there must have been mistaken. Well, now he'd be sure to discount anything else that witness had said, because she just couldn't be reliable.

He looked over at Ryan. The young, red-haired detective was flushed with embarrassment for not following up on the pharmacist days earlier. Inspector Davis had just reamed him out before pushing his way back onto Grove Street. Dozens of morning shoppers stood with their mouths open staring at Ryan, who was doing his best to melt into the sidewalk.

Elliot put aside his own annoyance and put his arm around Ryan's shoulder. "I've been looking at the research you did on Mr. Barkley. It's very good, but I have a few questions." The crowd did little to disperse, but they no longer looked shocked. They stood aside as Elliot guided Ryan back toward his car.

"How am I ever going to face those people again?"

"Don't worry. Knowing them, they'll think Davis was

wrong. Anyway you are young and inexperienced and are expected to make some mistakes."

"Will he tell Captain Jaeger?"

"Count on it. Expect a few lumps."

Ryan could barely open his mouth, his frown was so set. "Great. He'll probably demote me. And I deserve it."

Elliot didn't speak. There was really nothing he could do about this situation. But he wanted to get back into the groove of the investigation, so he pulled out his notebook. Somewhat reluctantly, Ryan took his own book out. "What did you want to ask me about? Or was that just a sympathy remark?"

The chip on this guy's shoulder was bigger than Elliot had thought. Dominique had warned him that Ryan felt inadequate at times because of Elliot and Dominique's past success. But that reaction was childish and wouldn't help matters. Besides, if this guy had done his work there was a possibility that he had information that Elliot needed and he wasn't about to let anything hold up his own investigation. "You checked into a side business that Garth ran."

"Yes. Was there something specific you wanted to know?" Ryan asked.

"How was he doing it?"

"You mean undercutting Logan?"

Elliot tried to nod patiently.

"Okay, it worked like this. There were some women who complained about the cost of styling at the salon. Most of them seem to be pretty well off, but a few would go for extra weeks or even months between cuts just because they were so expensive. Even so, they were unwilling to go someplace else." Ryan relaxed a bit, warming to his subject. "Garth had told them that he could give them trims in between, if they'd just come to his house. It would cost a fraction of what the salon rate was, but they couldn't tell anyone."

"How many women?"

Ryan smiled, the first honest one Elliot had ever seen on the man. "Only the young, pretty ones."

"Single?"

"That didn't seem to enter into the criteria. In fact, if they were struggling newlyweds, he pushed them more."

"How altruistic of him."

"Not really. My source estimates that seventy-five percent of them are sorry they'd ever met him."

"How reliable is your source?"

"Armond hated Garth, if that's what you mean. But Garth didn't keep it a secret from anyone but Logan. He bragged about a lot of nasty things he'd done over the years."

"So why didn't Logan find out?"

"I don't know."

"You didn't ask him?"

"I wasn't sure I should. It is a secret."

Elliot felt his anger boiling up again, but there was no point. He'd have a word with Dominique later about this kid, and let her handle it. Without saying anything else for fear he'd put the kid back into his blues, he turned and left, headed straight back for a chat with Logan. He only hoped that Davis hadn't found out about this latest slipup—he wanted to be ahead of him for a change.

Tillie's voice on the telephone held a trace of mirth. "We have a little mystery here, too," she said.

When Wally roused herself from her deep thoughts to answer the phone, she realized she was way behind on getting dinner ready. She hoped that whatever Tillie had to say would be quick, and wouldn't require a personal visit. "What is it?"

"Do you want to try to figure it out?"

"I think I have enough mysteries to work on right now. Why don't you tell me about it?"

"Okay. It isn't really anything, but it is kind of funny."

"Funny ha-ha or funny queer?"

"You decide. I've been helping Vivian set up a party."

"What is the occasion?"

"That's the thing. There is no occasion, but we are going to have a party anyway. We have more than enough money."

That sounded odd to Wally. "Are you okay?"

"Why do you ask, dear?"

"Maybe it's me. I thought I heard you say that you, that is the collective you, meaning people in your building, among the tightest on earth, may I remind you, have enough money for something?"

"We're not all that tight."

Wally had to agree. "You, that is, the personal you, are not tight. You are one of the most generous people I know. But the building as a spending force is tight."

"That's true. And that's actually the mystery."

"What is?"

"The party."

Wally was beginning to get stabbing pains behind her eyes as a headache crept over her. She also began to tune out. Tillie was not ordinarily vague, but possibly her years of living among the somewhat fuzzy and occasionally demented neighbors in that building were getting to her. Another possibility occurred to Wally, though, and hoping for the best, she tried a new line of questioning.

"Is the party one of those murder mystery parties where people act things out?"

"No, why do you ask?"

This conversation was getting to Wally in frustrating ways she'd never before experienced. Tillie was not known for being coy, or for toying with people, but here she was, making mincemeat out of Wally's brain. "I'm trying to find out what this party is all about."

"About? It isn't about anything."

"Tillie . . ."

"Sorry dear. It's going to be really good, actually. We're going to have deli, and someone suggested that maybe you could do something about dessert."

"Me? I hope you told that person that I'm very busy, with the wedding and all."

"Oh, the party isn't until after the wedding. You'll be done with school, too, by then, so you'll have plenty of time."

Wally wondered how Tillie felt so free to spend her time,

but she didn't comment. "I still don't understand what the mystery is."

"Pay attention. The mystery is: where did the money come from?"

"Where did it come from?" asked Wally. "Some anonymous donor?"

"No, don't be silly. Bingo."

"Did you think of it?"

"What are you talking about?"

"You said Bingo. I thought you just figured something out."

"Is that what you say?"

"When?"

"When you solve a mystery?"

"No. Are you going to explain this to me?"

"I'm sorry dear, I'm just having a little fun."

Which made exactly one of us, Wally thought. "Go ahead."

"Okay. As you may know, Gertie used to run the Bingo games."

"I remember."

"Then she got sick. She couldn't run them for a while, so Vivian took over. In four months she had enough profit to throw an all-expenses-paid party. Somehow Gertie never had any money left over. That's the mystery."

"You think Gertie has been pocketing the money?"

"That's the current thought."

"So what's the mystery?"

"I guess there isn't one, but we wondered who is going to talk to her about it."

There followed a pregnant pause, and before anything developed, Wally jumped right in. "You can't mean me? You don't want me to confront her, do you?"

Tillie sounded defensive. "We asked Dora, the lady in the office, you know, but she said she couldn't possibly. She gets hives."

"Hives?"

"From confrontation."

"Listen carefully, Tillie. I am not going to talk to Gertie about this. I have absolutely no standing to discuss it."

"But you're a detective."

"No, I'm not."

"Would you change your mind if I told you that Gertie has been saying she knows something about the murder case?"

"Does she?"

"She says it whenever we mention the party."

"Maybe she just wants to change the subject."

"But you see why you have to talk to her, don't you?"

Wally sighed. "Yes." As she hung up, she wondered, what else?

Chapter Fourteen

"Is it just me, or is it awfully quiet in here?" asked Eunice, blinking her long eyelashes.

Crystal looked around, waiting for someone to answer. No one did. But everyone knew that it was quiet because the biggest source of noise, both directly and indirectly, was now lying under a blanket of fresh sod in a park-like setting overlooking the Garden State Parkway.

Gossip had ground to a standstill and Crystal realized that a certain zing had gone out of her job. Garth's absence left the salon sagging.

For a while the speculation about Garth's murder had filled the hole, but lately that had petered out as well. There wasn't a single theory bouncing around. This job was getting boring.

Crystal sighed. It was only two o'clock and she'd hit the five-thirty doldrums. If only Ryan would stop by to break up the monotony. He was awfully cute, if overly serious, and Crystal kind of liked the way he kissed; sweet, and full of longing, as if he couldn't get enough. Their first date had gone incredibly well.

Eunice slipped out the back door on her way to suck a cancer stick and Crystal decided that she'd join her for a breath of fresh air. The air would be tinged with smoke, which was especially enticing, since Crystal still missed her own cigarettes, at least sometimes.

"I can't understand it," said Eunice, exhaling, savoring her Virginia Slim. "You would think that at least half of the people in that place would be so happy that Garth is gone"—she coughed—"not to speak ill of the dead, that they'd have a lot to say that they could never say in his presence because he'd mock them."

"You're right," Crystal agreed. "But he never bothered you, did he?"

Eunice snorted. "Lordy, no. He wouldn't dare. I knew his mother, you know." She took another long drag on her cigarette and let the smoke out slowly, through her nose. "Besides, he liked to pick his fights with the younger people."

"Are you saying that one of the people in the salon killed him?"

"I didn't say that hon, did I? And I promise, I don't know anything. But I'll tell you one thing. He sure made a lot of people mad, always having an opinion on every little thing anyone did, and also . . ."

"Also what?"

"Well, I just think that he didn't confine his viper's tongue to people in the salon. He was quite a talker, you remember, and he didn't care who listened." Eunice laughed. "He was like that since he was little. Always talking about every little thing, never heard of keeping a secret, except his own."

A crow swooped into the parking lot and picked at the carcass of a squirrel. Crystal shivered, despite the warm day.

"You know," said Eunice, "some of my customers used to complain about him, even though you would have thought they had nothing to do with him." She took another puff, narrowing one eye as the smoke billowed past. "He never wanted to work on the blue hairs, he always said. And he hated wrinkles."

"So why did they complain?"

"My ladies? Because he was such a big mouth, always bragging about something he did to somebody. He had no shame. And he never heard of 'don't kiss and tell.' My ladies got embarrassed sometimes when he talked about it. I even had one leave in the middle of a set, because she couldn't take it."

"Really?"

Eunice nodded. "It was amazing, let me tell you, although I don't remember what he said. Oh, wait, yes I do. But it's odd. It wasn't about women for a change, it was about something he did to someone in business, or something."

Crystal was really listening now. "Are you saying that whatever he did was related to the person who was in your chair?"

Eunice tilted her head. "I don't know . . ." She threw her cigarette onto the blacktop. "But I shouldn't speak ill of the dead, even if he was a son of Satan."

Wally wanted to find out what Dominique had learned about the blackmailing that Garth was apparently engaged in, as well as to see if she could help with Elliot's problem.

Dominique answered on the second ring, at about the same time as her husband, James. Wally said hello to both of them, and goodbye to James when he hung up.

"I was just going to call you," said Dominique. "I believe you are onto something. We've checked some bank records and it seems that Garth was a busy boy, squirreling away money from many different sources. He must have been extorting money from more people than we thought."

"So you're checking out all the blackmailing that Garth was involved in?"

"Yes," said Dominique. "I can say this much. We have several leads. Garth liked to keep records."

"How are we ever going to find out who killed him?"

"We're checking everything, and we keep getting new leads. Elliot is looking into a few himself, and if his boss checks, it'll be clear that he isn't twiddling his thumbs."

"Am I supposed to feel relieved?"

"I don't know. It's possible none will pan out." Dominique was quiet for a while.

Wally was beginning to wonder if she should say goodnight when Dominique sighed; it was long, loud and pregnant with meaning. Wally waited.

"Mrs. Morris?"

The use of her formal name surprised Wally, at the same

time that it warned her that what Dominique was about to say meant, among other things, trouble. Carefully letting out half her breath, she said, "Yes?"

"Um, uh, one of the leads we had is kind of up your alley."

Wally gulped. "And?"

"And I was wondering if you could check it out."

"Before I say yes, could you explain?"

"We still have questions about what one of those people in your mother-in-law's building saw. We were kind of hoping that you could talk to that person."

"Shouldn't one of you do that?"

"Oh, we did. She was very vague. We were kind of hoping you'd know what associations to make so she could answer."

"Who was it?"

"Gertie Irving."

Wally's stomach dropped. It was the same woman whom Tillie wanted her to question about the bingo money. "Oh."

"You know her?"

"Let's just say you aren't the first person who wants me to talk to her."

"Really? Why?"

"I guess you could say because she knows about things that other people are wondering about."

"Do you think she's capable of answering?"

"I don't know. She's either capable, or pretty much in a fog. I'm really not sure which. But I'll look into the situation."

"There's just one thing," said Dominique. "No one can know."

"Why doesn't that surprise me? But don't worry. I have a whole other reason to be speaking to her, and no one will know."

"Gertie," said Wally, for the second time. The old woman beside her kept turning away, every time she asked about the missing bingo money. The term 'barking up the wrong tree' came to Wally's mind again. Gertie was beyond vague.

Wally touched the papery skin of Gertie's arm. Faded blue

eyes met hers. "I'm sorry, I just don't know," she said. "I thought I put it away carefully."

Suddenly she broke down in tears. 'Inconsolable' was too gentle a word for Gertie's distress, and four women who had obviously been listening at the door burst into the apartment and pushed Wally aside.

"What are you doing to her?" asked Pearl. "Why did you make her cry?"

"You know what she did," said Shirley. "You heard the whole thing. She badgered her about the missing money, and about that murder."

Another woman, whose name Wally didn't know, put her knobby fingered hand to her lips. "Shh. She isn't supposed to know we were listening."

"Oh," said Shirley, with her right arm akimbo. She seemed to want to put her left hand on her other hip, but it didn't work, because of her cane. Instead, she pointed her cane at Wally. "Like she can't figure that out. Don't you know who this is? She's a detective, like Jessica Fletcher."

"She's not as tall as Jessica Fletcher," said one of the others, "or as old."

"Look who's calling someone old."

Gertie put up her hand. "Please stop. Let me talk to Wally alone."

Wally looked at her, puzzled, but saw a clarity in her eyes that she hadn't seen earlier. "I promise I won't upset her again," Wally said. "I just want to find out a few things."

The ladies left, slowly, turning back several times on their way to the door to check on Gertie and shoot Wally threatening looks. Finally they were outside, although the door was still cracked open, and Wally could faintly hear Shirley's raspy breathing. She got a drink of water for Gertie from the kitchen, handed it to her, and sat back down on the plastic-covered couch to wait for her to speak.

"I am very sorry," said Gertie. "I didn't steal the money. I just can't keep track of it. I should have told them when they asked me to be in charge of the bingo money that I'm not very good at it." She took another sip of her water. "My son has to take care of my money, you know. He thought it was strange that I was handling money for the building. He told me not to do it, but I just couldn't admit that I can't . . ." She broke off, tears again threatening to fall.

Wally put her hand on the old lady's liver-spotted wrist. "Do you know where the money is?"

Gertie shook her head. "I have no idea. I was keeping it so carefully, and I don't know what happened."

"Where did you keep it?"

Gertie pointed to a small desk. "In that drawer."

"May I look?"

"I guess."

Wally walked over to the desk and pulled open the top drawer. As she did, she felt something catch and she shut the drawer a little, then slid it open again. There was no longer anything caught, and she looked to see what it might have been.

The drawer was almost empty. There were a few papers in it, at the bottom, but otherwise, nothing.

"Are you sure this is the one?"

"Yes. It's the only one I can even open in the desk. And I know it's empty. I just don't know why."

Wally slid the drawer back in and turned, out of ideas. But for some reason the drawer didn't feel quite right. She looked at it, and found it sticking out. Even when she pushed, it did not go all the way in.

A thought occurred to her, and she pulled the drawer out, all the way. Looking inside, she knew she had solved another mystery. The back of the drawer space was stuffed with dollar bills.

"Gertie, I think I found the money."

"What?"

Wally pitched her voice louder. "I said, I think I found the money." She stooped down, and reaching in, pulled out a wad of bills. She had to do it several times, and pull out the other drawers, which wasn't easy. Each one had bills of several denominations behind it. When she was done, the floor was covered in money.

"Please clean up that mess, dear," said Gertie, staring myopically at the money. "My cleaning lady won't be here until Thursday."

"It's the money, Gertie."

The door burst open before Gertie could react.

"You found it!" said Pearl, waddling over to the pile.

"Tillie's daughter-in-law is a genius!" Shirley shouted into the hallway. She spoke to the other woman. "Stay here, Greta. Tell them when they come." Greta stood dutifully by the door, as people shouted to one another and came toward the apartment.

Gertie was crying again. "You see, it wasn't my fault. I put the money away, but it kept vanishing."

Pearl had a disgusted look on her face, but she soothed Gertie anyway. "It's okay, problem solved," she cooed. "Don't worry about it anymore."

Wally couldn't understand how the woman had not realized that the drawer was eating the money, but she could see one thing clearly: she wasn't going to get any more information out of Gertie, at least not right away. She excused herself, threading her way out of the apartment, which was now full of women who had arrived in a progression of canes and walkers, and down the equally crowded hallway to the door.

Chapter Fifteen

In the diner, Rita Barkley sat across the table from Elliot. It was the middle of her work day and she wore her aerobics outfit with a spandex tank top and shorts. Her brown pony tail was pulled up high on her head, making her look younger than her mid-thirties. She was in excellent shape.

After showing Elliot her new engagement ring, Rita looked around. She wrinkled her nose and shook her head. "I can't believe I'm back in this God-forsaken dump. I see it hasn't changed at all. They still have the same wallpaper and those fake ferns are so disgusting."

Elliot let her ramble on, although he listened carefully. While he really had no hope that she'd be able to help him with the investigation, he was running out of ideas. Since Rita was the first of a long line of ex-wives that Garth had left strewn along the way, he hoped she'd have some information for him, or at least say something to give him a lead. "You didn't seem too unhappy at his funeral."

She flashed Elliot a broad grin. "I was positively ecstatic. I can't remember a nicer day, can you?"

"I, uh . . ."

"Of course," she said, leaning forward to reveal her ample cleavage, "it would have made more sense to have him cremated. He's gonna be burning forever, you know."

Elliot shifted in his seat, trying to hide the shivers her remark sent down his spine. "So I've heard. But what I want to know is, was there anyone you can think of who might have wanted to accelerate the process?"

"I can think of several people who had good reasons, including Sally and Tess. Although I doubt that either one of them would want to kill the father of their daughters. Besides," she added, while stirring her iced coffee, "Sally still hoped that Garth would come back to her and Madeline. But there was no way Garth would ever do that. Sally must have gained fifty pounds since he married her and he never had much use for Madeline. Lisa was the child he preferred."

"I had heard that he was violent," Elliot said.

"I'll say. I once heard him say to Sally that if she didn't lose the weight, he'd knock it off her. He absolutely hated fat people."

Elliot filed that tidbit in the back of his mind. He decided to see if any of Garth's recent paramours may have been dropped due to weight gain.

To Rita he said, "All of Garth's ex-wives have solid alibis. I wasn't really expecting any information about them. What I'm really looking for is someone Garth hurt whom we wouldn't know about."

Rita squirmed in her seat in the booth. Crossing one leg over the other, she pondered the problem. Elliot struggled to keep his eyes off what he could see of her tanned legs. She looked Elliot right in the eye and said, "Do you have about a week? I've known, or at least I knew, Garth since grade school. He screwed up someone's life at least once a week. There were more kids seeing shrinks because of him than there were teachers in the school. And some of the teachers probably spent a few hours on a couch too."

Elliot did not see the connection between the bully teenager and his choice of profession. It seemed hard to believe that someone who was to become a hairdresser could have wielded so much power.

Rita seemed to read his mind. "You're wondering about his career. Well, believe me, it wasn't his first choice."

"Oh?"

"Garth originally wanted to be an actor." Rita giggled. "But when he tried out for the school play he froze, I mean solid. So he gave up his plans for Hollywood on the spot. Then he decided to really do something with his swimming ability. But there was a faster boy who kept Garth in second place. Even when he was disqualified, poor guy, can you believe . . . Oh, you didn't know him. Anyway, Garth didn't show any great potential, at least not enough to get a scholarship.

"He needed money for college, so that summer, after graduation, he worked at the country club pool as a lifeguard. Apparently he caught the eye of one of the young married women. Her husband traveled almost every week. She ended up losing her husband and then her ability to give Garth money, which is basically what he was after, and which was why he dropped her. Other lonely women filled in and by the end of the summer he had decided to stay in town and forget college. So he took a job in a hair salon, liked it, especially the perks that seemed to keep coming his way, and he went to beauty school."

Rita leaned forward and sipped her drink through the straw. "I haven't said anything shocking, so you must be so silent because you are trying to figure out why I married the creep."

Elliot cleared his throat and raised his eyebrows.

"I'll take that as a question. I married him because I was totally stupid. Although you haven't asked, I'm sure you want to know—he married me because it was convenient. One of the many women he was involved with decided to leave her husband for Garth, and he was in no way interested in having that happen. I was just the innocent dupe who happened to be available, since I'd been dumped by my boyfriend. Garth looked pretty good at the time, even though my mother didn't agree." She sighed. "We actually had about a week of good times until the real ogre emerged, with an upper cut to my jaw. And then my stubbornness enabled me to put up with more of that for four years."

Elliot felt sorry for her. "Who else did Garth hurt?"

"Let me think. Every pretty girl in high school, except the real egg-heads who had more sense, many of the boys, both physically and mentally, by the way. He had quite a vicious tongue." She cocked her head to one side. "I'd say, just about everyone. This doesn't help, does it?"

"Not really."

"I'm sorry. My fiancé told me that I wouldn't be able to help you, but I didn't listen. He's a really good guy, you should meet him."

"Oh? Does he know something about the case?"

Rita narrowed her eyes and scowled. "I can see you're totally focused. No, sorry. He's just a good guy. Well, I've got to go."

She popped out of the booth, and grabbed her bag before running out the door. Elliot didn't even try not to watch her spandex shorts as she left.

Chapter Sixteen

On Monday Wally knew she had to go back to see Gertie. There was still unfinished business between them. Tillie had initially advised giving her a few more days, explaining that she had recovered from the excitement of finding the bingo money, but had been thrown back into a funk by the sweepstakes incident.

"What sweepstakes?" Wally had asked.

Tillie giggled. "Well, you know how when you get a sweepstakes solicitation they put your name in it and it kind of looks like you personally won?"

"Yes." Wally remembered. Hers had said, *Voltairine Morris, if you have the winning numbers, you have won the grand prize!* "So what happened?"

"Gertie thought she won ten million dollars," said Tillie. "She called her son to come take her to collect her money and it took a long time for him to explain that she hadn't. When she finally understood, Gertie was mighty embarrassed since she had also told everyone in the building that she won."

That was Saturday. By now there was nothing to stop Wally's return visit. Gertie had promised to be home all morning. But questioning a woman who was so easily confused seemed likely to be a waste of time.

Wally knocked on Gertie's door as loudly as she could

without bruising her knuckles. After three minutes, the woman answered.

Standing, Gertie was even shorter than Wally. Her back had a distinct curve and she leaned heavily on her cane. Her bluish gray hair, however, was freshly set and sprayed.

"Your hair looks lovely," Wally said.

"Thank you. The girl just left. She does an even better job than any of the beauty parlors, don't you think?"

"You don't go to Resplendence anymore?"

A tinge of regret clouded Gertie's face. "No."

Wally followed her inside and, doing as she was told, sat on the plastic covered couch. Although she had seen the plastic the last time she was in this apartment, she'd had forgotten about it and had worn shorts. She dreaded the thought of standing up when she had to leave.

Gertie handed her a glass of iced tea. "I really haven't thanked you for helping me. I thought I was losing my mind and I just couldn't tell anyone. I admit it was kind of ridiculous not to realize where the bingo money was going, but I had begun to think that I was sleep walking or something."

Seeing her calm smile, Wally launched into her questions. "Tell me what you know about the murder."

"I know I don't see well, but I am not blind."

She paused. Wally waited.

"I am very upset with the police," Gertie continued. "They don't seem to believe that I saw what I saw."

"You said you saw Dr. Fisch."

"I did."

"You said you saw *Doctor* Fisch. He isn't a doctor, he is a pharmacist."

Gertie looked at her, her pale blue eyes unwavering. She cocked her head to one side and said, "Whatever. How can you be sure I didn't see him?"

"He's been in Hawaii. You would have had to have exceptional vision."

Gertie leaned back in her chair, as if she'd had a revelation. "So that's why they don't believe I saw those other people?"

"It didn't check out."

Gertie stood up, although it was hard to tell. She was still bent in various places. "You don't have to believe me either," she said. The face of defeat that she had worn before the missing money was found had returned.

"I-I-uh, I don't disbelieve you. Please don't think . . ."

"Maybe you should go."

That was the last thing Wally wanted to do, stuck as she was by sweat to the plastic. The noise would be deafening as her thighs de-sucked themselves. But she had no choice. Gertie was steaming toward the front door, and she'd eventually get there, open it, and expect Wally to leave. As quickly as she could, Wally stood up.

Although she knew her face was bright red from the embarrassing noise that ensued, she stammered a goodbye to Gertie, and left. She'd call Tillie later, she decided, rather than stop by on her way home.

"I'm sorry, Dominique," Wally said, when she called the police station later that afternoon. "I don't really think we got anything useable. Gertie just thought that I should know that her eye-witness account should not be so easily dismissed."

Dominique sighed loudly enough for Wally to hear through the phone. "We checked everything out, Wally. As you pointed out, Mr. Fisch has been out of town, and those delivery people that Gertie saw couldn't have been there. Just as an example, there was no UPS delivery on the day of the murder."

"Do you have any other leads?"

"We're following up on a few things, but nothing that I'm holding out great hope for. We'll have to go back and start over, I think. But thanks for trying."

There was nothing to do now but wait for something to turn up.

Wally just hated that.

As soon as school let out the next day, Wally sent herself back to Tillie's building. She hoped that she wouldn't run into too many of the residents, she needed time to get over her meeting with Gertie. She'd once had a fifth grade teacher who had looked at her in the dismissive way that Gertie had the day before, and she'd hated that every bit as much as getting her teeth drilled.

That concept was close to home today particularly. Tillie had decided that it was time to have her dentures relined before the wedding. "I don't want them to slip out, you know," she'd said, when Wally said, "Why don't you wait until your foot is healed?"

Her answer had not really been one, but Tillie's conviction was so strong that even though Nate had to teach another seminar and it meant that Wally had to take Tillie to the dentist, she'd insisted.

"You can go do whatever and just pick me up when it's convenient," Tillie said as they walked into the medical building.

"It's okay," said Wally. "I really have nothing to do today." That wasn't entirely true, but worrying about the murder being solved in time for the wedding didn't seem to be a good enough reason to run around town. "I'll just read some magazines."

They rode up to the third floor of the building with two other people. Each of them made a wide berth around Tillie and had pitying looks on their faces. Tillie winked at Wally. When the people were out of earshot, she whispered, "People treat me like an invalid with no ability to speak for myself."

"No they don't," Wally argued. "I'm sure you're wrong."

"Hi," said the receptionist, looking directly at Wally as she helped Tillie into the dentist's office. "How are you today?"

Hearing no response from beside her and feeling that one was required, Wally said, "Fine."

Still looking at Wally, the receptionist said, "What can we do for you today?"

Expecting Tillie to give her name, Wally said nothing. But Tillie didn't speak either, so Wally answered. "This is Mrs. Morris. She is here to see the dentist."

"Tell her to have a seat." The receptionist darted away.

Wally turned to Tillie. "Why didn't you speak up?"

"She wasn't talking to me."

"Don't get haughty. You're bringing this on yourself."

"I didn't start. She did."

The receptionist was back, again looking directly at Wally. "Bring her in here."

Wally helped Tillie into the chair. The dentist came in and looked at Tillie's cane, and her leg, and said, "Were you out dancing again, Mrs. Morris? I told you that moshing was not safe for a woman of your age." Tillie beamed with pleasure that she had been reinstated to personhood.

"I didn't do it dancing," she said. "I was skiing."

"Oh. I should have known. Please open." He reached his hand in and took hold of the top denture.

Wally, who was sitting opposite her mother-in-law on one of those little wheel around stools, turned her attention outside. She did not want to see Tillie without her teeth.

It was an interesting view of the parking lot. All the cars looked like elongated rectangles, and there were so many, constantly coming and going. Wally felt like a voyeur, especially when she witnessed a young couple fighting, slamming doors, stalking away from each other and finally, after the girl broke down in tears, reconciling.

Shortly after that, and after Tillie rinsed her very empty mouth and lay back to rest while the dentist worked on her dentures, a delivery truck drove up. There was no mistaking the brown truck, although Wally was surprised that the roof was translucent, not solid as she'd always assumed.

The truck parked right in front, where Wally had let Tillie out, and stayed there for a long time. The driver only carried one small package, and Wally wondered why he just didn't park in another space so that handicapped people had access to the doorway.

Whenever Wally looked up from reading her magazine the parking lot looked different. People came and went and it began to get full. A car pulled into the driveway and wound around among the parked cars searching for a spot. Wally laughed to herself, realizing that she had the perfect view of the lot, and could have directed the car from above. Finally a spot was found and the driver got out and came into the building.

A moment later, the UPS driver came out. Wally looked at her watch and realized that forty minutes and several refittings of Tillie's dentures had passed while he was inside. Wally expected to see the driver burdened with a lot of packages, since he was in the building for so long, but he came out empty-handed.

"There goes Ricky," someone said.

"He's late," said another voice.

Wally turned to see who was talking. It was the receptionist, looking over her shoulder, and one of the nurses. "It's a record," she added, looking at her watch.

The puzzled look on Wally's face must have been evident, because the nurse explained. "Ricky hates the gas station. He uses the bathroom on the first floor. He's very regular." The two women laughed out loud as each went back to work.

"Now, Tillie," said the dentist, "how is that?"

Tillie chomped down. "Good."

"Good. Give my regards to your granddaughter." With a wave, he was gone.

Wally didn't know which she liked least—being Tillie's spokesperson, or her invisible helper.

Chapter Seventeen

Crystal got to the salon earlier than she ever had and realized that a whole world of activity took place before her usual arrival. She was aware, naturally, that several people came in at the crack of dawn, because she'd seen the bills for their visits, but until that moment she had never seen them nor fully appreciated who they were.

One of those people was Roxanna Donner. On paper, where her daily visits were recorded for billing purposes, she seemed innocuous enough, but in person she was nothing short of insufferable. She reminded Crystal of the worst of the girls she'd hated in high school, the ones in the most popular group, the rich ones. It hadn't been that many years since Crystal, a key member of the second most popular group, the one whose members were from more modest backgrounds, felt stung by some of their words.

It made her cringe, watching Roxanna. But what Crystal really couldn't figure out was how Logan, who of all people was one of the most demanding and least likely to make himself subservient, could stand the high school girl's imperious and often whiny tones. His white Ben Casey style shirt hung partially open, having been thrown on hastily, and he seemed extremely tense.

"My hair looks terrible," Roxanna whined, staring at her reflection in the mirror. She moved her head from side to side, still keeping her eyes focused on the mirror. "It has no life. Can't you do something?"

Logan put down his blow dryer and the large rounded brush he was holding. He smiled, a forced effort at best. "Your hair looks beautiful, as usual. Have you been using the shampoo and conditioner I gave you?"

Crystal had to laugh, although she kept it to herself. 'Gave' was not exactly what he had done. He had charged her father, on the weekly bill, seventy-five dollars for six ounces of shampoo. The conditioner had been less expensive, but there were only three ounces in the bottle. No matter how concentrated they were, they were expensive hair products.

"Yes," said Roxanna, pouting at the mirror. "I did for a while, but I didn't like the smell. I threw it out."

Crystal winced. She watched as Logan, gritting his teeth, came around to the front of the chair that Roxanna occupied. For a second, Crystal was afraid that he was going to slap the brat, but all he did was look at the front of her hair closely.

"Perhaps we can highlight it some more," he said. "But not now, or you'll be late for school. Can you come back afterwards?"

"With all those other people?" Roxanna sneered. "No way. I'll come early tomorrow."

"You'd have to come in at five-thirty to get it done before school."

"So? I can sleep while it's processing."

Crystal knew that there was no way that Logan would come in that early. She waited for his refusal.

"That's true," said Logan. "Good idea, I'll see you then." He walked Roxanna to the door with his arm around her shoulder in a paternal fashion. "Have a good day."

As soon as she left, he went into his office and slammed the door. Two other women, also early blow-dry customers, both of Jordan, stared after him. One, who had already finished being blown and was grabbing a second cup of coffee before heading for her train to New York, looked at Crystal. "I don't know why he puts up with that child."

The other, who had just finished putting milk and artificial sweetener into her own cup of coffee before sitting down in Jordan's chair said, "Tell me you don't know."

The first woman stopped in her tracks. "Oh, of course, what was I thinking?" She laughed, and pushed the door open, disappearing into the morning air.

Crystal was totally perplexed. With the hope that she could find out why her boss put up with Roxanna, she picked up her clip board and edged closer to Jordan's chair.

"That girl is such a brat," said the woman in the chair. Her damp hair, which had been in a clip when she came in to keep it off her clothes, hung limply around her plastic smock covered shoulders.

Jordan, whose T-shirt today was the tightest one yet since his surgery so that everyone could see how flat his stomach was, nodded at her in the mirror while combing her hair straight. "I think she has single handedly caused his ulcer."

Crystal counted the bottles of hair spritz at the station next to Jordan, while trying to look as if she didn't hear a thing.

The woman nodded back at Jordan in the mirror. "Of course, his gambling debts could be another cause."

Jordan snorted. "If Ted Donner hadn't bailed out Logan, he would have lost the salon. Putting up with his daughter is a small enough price to pay for Logan to keep his business." Jordan picked up his blower. Finger on the trigger, he added, "When I think that this place could close in two seconds if Donner were to pull out, I positively get chills." Shivering for emphasis, he switched on the blower, and Crystal, who couldn't have heard any more in any case, went back to her counter.

The conversation had shaken her to the core. Besides wondering if she should be looking for another job, she wondered how she could have been oblivious to the situation. And it didn't add up. Why would Mr. Donner pay vast sums of money for Roxanna to come have her hair blown dry if he was a partner? She had to find a way to get into Logan's books.

She sighed. She might as well be trying to find a way to have a picnic on the moon.

* * *

"What've you got?" asked Marshall. The assistant prosecutor sat behind his desk with his hands fully extended, pushing against it. That made his shoulders look even larger, and his shirt buttons strained against the fabric. "It's been weeks already and so far I haven't heard you caught the killer."

That his boss was angry came as no surprise to Elliot. "No, sir," he said, wishing the lump in his stomach would go away. It was no use pointing out that it wasn't his job to find a killer, not any more. Marshall was expecting him to do it, or at least help Davis to do it. The case had a high profile, even more so since the IRS started making a lot of noise about the details of the Barkley bank accounts.

"I expected more of you. Maybe we made a mistake." Marshall stood up and looked out his office window, giving Elliot time to wonder if his job was in jeopardy.

He used that time to figure out the best presentation of the facts as he knew them. Sooner or later Marshall would stop the theatrics and want an accounting. Hoping that his voice would come out without cracking, but unwilling to cough and clear his throat, Elliot launched into his report.

"We have eliminated as suspects most of the people known to be in the area of the murder on that day. There were so many people around that almost every one of them has an alibi. Allowing for confusion, however, we have retained, on our list, the following people." As he paused, he allowed himself the throat clearing cough. "Logan Fletcher is top on our list."

"Motive?"

"He made Garth a partner in the salon, without a financial investment."

"Did Barkley bring anything to the party?"

"Nothing concrete. We are looking into the finances. As you can imagine, Fletcher is not forthcoming. There may have been some sort of extortion or blackmail involved."

"To hell with him. Get a subpoena if you have to."

"We have applied for one." Elliot looked over his notes, even though he knew exactly what they said. "We are still checking on a few other people. Unfortunately, the forensics information has so far been useless. There was hair from many people, no unexplained fingerprints, and even Barkley was wearing gloves at the time, so he didn't pick up any skin fragments in the struggle."

"Why on earth was the victim wearing gloves?"

"Apparently he was about to do a color job when he went into the consultation room."

"Where was the person whose hair he was about to color? Maybe she's our killer."

"She is a one hundred ten pound great-grandmother," said Elliot. "I don't think she could have done it, even if she was not having her hair washed at the time. She was still waiting for him at the sink when the body was found."

"Does that help us establish the time of the stabbing better?"

"She's not sure how long she was there. Mr. Barkley insisted on personally escorting his clients into the cubicle, but was not known for doing it promptly. She assumed he was making a phone call or something. And the hair washer was no help at all at pinpointing the time. Mrs. Morris's estimate is still the one we're using."

Marshall looked over the files on his desk. "I guess, based on the evidence, that the person who struggled with and stabbed Barkley must have been strong. He was a big guy. No woman could have done that."

"Well, she would have had to have been very strong, if it was a woman," Elliot agreed. "Davis is convinced it was a man."

"And you don't agree?"

"I don't want to eliminate any possibilities, just because of stereotypes."

Marshall leaned forward as if ready to reach for Elliot's throat. "How broad-minded of you." Then, sitting back in his chair, he added, "No pun intended."

No mirth detected, thought Elliot.

"So you think it was a woman?" asked Marshall.

"I didn't say that."

"Just what are you saying?" Marshall was on his feet. "Do you have any idea who killed Garth Barkley?"

"The man had a lot of people angry at him," said Elliot. "Many of them were women. At the same time, many of those women had relationships with other men. One of them may have done this."

"Do you believe that? Do you have a lead?"

Elliot held up open hands. "I don't have anything concrete."

"Don't leave here until you do."

"I beg your pardon?"

Marshall shook his head, and looked at Elliot as if he were an idiot. "I don't mean you have to stay in your office until you find the murderer. Unless he's under your desk, you wouldn't find him there, would you?"

Logan looked worse than he had since the day of the murder. His face was chalk white, and he was sweating even in the frigid salon.

Crystal became even more worried. "You should, like, go see a doctor," she said, as Logan walked past her. "You had two cancellations and you don't have to be back here for an hour and a half."

Logan snorted. "Great, who canceled?"

"Mrs. MacLean and Mrs. Glazer."

"Why?" he asked, his voice strained.

Crystal looked into his watery eyes and felt sorry for the tyrant. "There is something at their children's nursery school today, and they had to go."

"They didn't know about this before?"

Crystal shrugged. She watched as Logan went to the computer and looked up his doctor's phone number, crossing her fingers with the hope that he'd be gone for a while. When he hung up, he took his car keys out of his pocket and mumbled something Crystal took to mean he'd see her later. She kept her eye on the street in front of the salon, waiting for Logan's car to pull out of the back lot and drive past, and, as soon as he did, she got Lexie to cover the desk.

"Where are you going?" Lexie asked.

"Don't ask." Crystal checked to see who was looking and, when it seemed everyone was busy with something else, went into Logan's office.

She looked for his financial records, for anything that would point to Mr. Donner being a backer of the salon. Unfortunately, she didn't know Logan's password for the computer on his desk. So she accessed what she was privy to—the billing records. Looking under Donner, she found the records of Roxanna's daily blow-outs. The one for last month, which, due to the addition of the shampoo and conditioner was a much higher amount than the others, was the one she was trying to trace.

The bill was cleared on the twenty-eighth, and Crystal checked the bank deposit for that day. Not finding an entry for the amount on the bill, she tried the credit card vouchers. There was also no entry for that. It appeared that the bill was cleared only in theory, not in reality.

While it was not proof that Mr. Donner was a financial partner, it was a clue. Crystal wondered what to do about that. Maybe she should tell Ryan. Maybe he would know what to do.

Chapter Eighteen

The phone rang and Elliot picked it up on the first ring. "Levine."

"Scott," said Dominique's perky voice. "I think my little Ryan may have stumbled onto something."

Elliot listened to an explanation about Ted Donner, another of Logan Fletcher's silent partners. Actual cash was involved, giving him a renewed sense of hope that some logical trail could be found between the victim and his killer. Donner also happened to be the owner of the property that the photography studio occupied, which itself was an interesting coincidence. Or was it? "Did you say that he is Roxanna's father?"

"Yes," said Dominique. "We're checking his alibi. But I thought you might like to talk to Logan again and ask him about this."

"I will."

"Good," said his former partner, sounding more energized. But she sounded less confident a second later when she added, "Elliot?"

"What?"

"We should tell Davis, shouldn't we?"

That was one depressing thought, but unavoidable, Elliot realized. "Yes."

"I'm going to leave that up to you," said Dominique. "I told someone at the prosecutor's office, namely you, and I don't have to call him myself."

Elliot detected a considerable amount of tension in Dom's voice. "Are you scared of him?"

"No. I'm just hoping to give myself a little time to get some answers before he treats me like a moron again."

"Has he done that?"

"Not is so many words, but, well, you know him."

Elliot did, and he wondered what sitting on the information would cost him. But he wanted to do a little investigating first.

"We got a divorce." Wally's ears perked up at that statement, made by a woman in the booth behind her. She didn't turn around to see who said it, but contrived to see the woman's reflection in one of the dozen or so mirrors that were on the walls of the restaurant.

Wally had been early for her meeting with Elliot's mother. This juicy conversation behind her, by a woman whom, in spite of the distortions of the mirror, looked to be well coifed, casually dressed and about 65, might just serve as enough of a diversion while Wally waited. She didn't feel embarrassed in the least, but she made sure to keep a straight face so no one else would know she was listening.

"What do you mean?" asked the woman's lunch partner, someone with whom she seemed well-matched.

"I mean, you remember when Logan was in East Orange? That was ages ago, before everyone moved here. Well I had been going to him then, and . . ."

She was interrupted by her companion. "I went to him too. That was about twenty years ago, right?"

"No, longer. Maybe thirty-five."

"Yes. He was about twenty years old then. And pleasant, not arrogant like he's been lately. He used to care about people's hair back then." Wally could hear her rattling her coffee cup, which was followed by an slurp. "Ooh, this is so hot," the woman complained.

"Oh, so you know about how awful Logan became."

The coffee cup rattled back to its saucer. "Of course. The last time I went to him . . ."

Her inquisitive friend didn't bother waiting for her to finish the sentence. "Was that when he was at Hair Palace?"

"No, here in Grosvenor, but before he expanded. Well, the last time I went I told him I didn't like my hair, and he told me to learn to live with it."

"I noticed he didn't learn to live with his salon," said the first woman whose voice sounded vaguely familiar. It was driving Wally crazy that she couldn't turn around and see who these two women were. "He sure put a lot of money into it."

Another noisy sip was followed by a speculative, "I wonder where he got it. I wouldn't have thought he'd have that much, especially since that was right about the time his twins would have been in college."

"I heard he had a silent partner," said that familiar voice again. An indistinct image started to creep into Wally's mind. She could practically match the unseen face with the voice. "You don't think it was that Garth who was," she practically whispering, "murdered, do you?"

The coffee cup clattered down again as the waitress walked toward their table with a pot of coffee. Wally took the opportunity to catch a glimpse of the two women while she pretended to check the front door for her lunch date. She didn't recognize coffee cup lady, but the interrupting companion was Sybil, the busy-body former neighbor of her mother-in-law. Wally made sure she didn't get a chance to see her face. She didn't feel like answering personal questions about "the poor widow, Tillie."

"Some people do," Sybil's friend said, "but I heard Garth didn't have that kind of money. I heard the partner was someone rich, whom Logan knew back in the old days."

Sybil snorted. "So you went to someone else for your hair?"

"Wouldn't you?"

Chuckling, Sybil said, "I'm not so smart. I kept going to him until last year. Then I said enough. It's like a divorce."

"You washed him out of your hair, huh?"

Raucous laughter erupted. Wally tried not to smirk.

The waitress brought slices of pie to the women's table and poured them even more coffee. When she left, the woman who stopped going to Logan a long time ago said, "Your hair looks very pretty now."

"Thanks. I have it done at . . ."

Wally was unable to hear where the good styling was done because at that moment Elliot's mother, Cynthia, arrived at her table.

She looked at Wally curiously. "Do you have a back ache?" she asked, after greeting Wally and sitting down.

"No, why?"

"You looked like you were leaning a strange way, sort of backwards."

"Oh, no," said Wally, hoping that her face was not as red as it felt. "I was just stretching a bit. I have to bend a lot at the nursery school, you know."

Cynthia didn't look convinced. But she let it go.

Wally felt a warm feeling for this woman who would soon be related to her by marriage. Since the announcement of the wedding, the two women had been very happy working together on the plans. Later they were going to their fittings for the gowns they would wear, since they had chosen the same place to buy their dresses. It was a good sign for the future of the relationship.

"Elliot, I have a question," said Wally. She had placed the call to his office as soon as she arrived home.

There was an inward rush of air on Elliot's end of the line. "Didn't things go well at lunch with my mother?"

"What? Oh, yes. They were fine. We got our dresses and all that. We even finished the seating arrangements and sent the list to the calligrapher to make the table cards. But what I want to know is, did you know that Logan had funding from another source?"

"Uh, what did you hear?"

"Actually, it's what I overheard; that Logan may have a silent partner."

"I believe that's correct."

"You're being closed-mouthed."

"Sorry," said Elliot. "There is a lot of pressure."

"I'd like to help, but I can't if I don't know anything."

Elliot's lips were apparently sealed. But Wally felt his silence indicated that he wished there was something he could say.

"Let me ask you something," she said. "You still don't have a strong motive for Logan, do you? Even though he's your prime suspect?"

Silence was the only answer to her question.

That didn't stop Wally. "Would you have one if you knew that somehow Garth was jeopardizing Logan's partnership?"

Elliot still didn't say anything, but Wally took that as a 'yes.' "So you can't tell me, and I can't . . ." She stopped. "Unless it's Ted Donner."

Stunned was the only way Wally could describe Elliot's reaction. He could barely sputter out a question.

"There is a picture hanging in the corridor of the salon of Ted and Logan wearing uniforms," Wally explained. "I figured they were old friends, and Ted is wealthy. Maybe he helped Logan out with the financing. Am I right?"

Elliot sighed. "It is Ted Donner. Do you know him?"

"Sure," said Wally. "His daughter, Roxanna, was a student of mine many years ago. He's pretty well known around town, too, and not generally well liked. Didn't you know that?"

"I did," said Elliot, leaving Wally wondering if she had sounded like she was putting him down. "But," Elliot added, "we haven't yet found the important connection."

"So," said Wally, "all we have to do is prove that there was a threat to the investment, and that Logan had to kill Garth to prevent that."

Elliot didn't sound positive when he said, "Possibly. Or maybe . . ."

Wally put on her most confident tone. "You keep looking, and I'll do what I can."

But, after hanging up, Wally was faced with a problem.

Although she knew Ted Donner, she had no idea how to get the needed information.

It was time to visit Crystal.

"I think your bangs, like, need a trim," said Crystal, when Wally told her the kind of information she needed to get. "Eunice would be good at that."

"Can't I wait until Tillie comes in for her weekly appointment?" Wally asked, understanding what Crystal was getting at, but unwilling to sacrifice her bangs for the cause. There was nothing she hated more than too short bangs, and she had been trimming them herself for weeks, trying to wait until the perfect time before the wedding for her official haircut.

"No, they are really too long." Crystal led her over to Eunice's chair, and explained about the trim. "I was just saying to Wally that you've known Logan for years, through all of his salon changes and improvements. She was wondering about the renovations."

Eunice narrowed her blue-shadowed, long-lashed eyes and coolly assessed both Wally and Crystal. "I'm gonna need an extra long break after this trim," she warned, fingering the pack of cigarettes in her pocket. "Make sure I have no appointments."

After Crystal went back to the desk, Eunice fussed with Wally's cape as if she were going to be spray painted. "I don't mind explaining this to you," she whispered, "because I know you know how to be discreet."

"Thanks. I guess my big question is, after all these years, why did Logan need a partner to provide a infusion?"

Eunice lowered her head and peered at Wally over the top of her half-glasses. In her gravelly voice she whispered, "Atlantic City."

"Oh." Wally knew what was implied. "So he got money from Ted to cover his gambling debts?"

"Yes. Ted Donner is the only one in the partnership with money. I hear he's loaded."

Wally had heard that, too. But Ted Donner was notoriously

tight-fisted in business. He always ordered the cheapest building materials that would meet code on the new apartments he seemed to have continually springing up on every vacant piece of land in the county. He hired the cheapest labor and required the contractors to give back a percentage to him, or lose his business.

Twice Nate had turned down Ted's insurance business, saying that he wasn't taking on new clients. But Wally knew that it was because on a least one occasion there had been a suspicion of wrongdoing in a building fire.

That was just the opposite of how Ted was with his own personal consumption and that of his family. Ted Donner was a natty and obviously expensive dresser with diamond rings on each of his pinkies. So were his wife and daughter, the latter Wally remembered as being obnoxious, even as a four-year-old. "How did Logan get him to lend him the money?"

"Ted and Logan were old army buddies. They both got drafted right after high school. I have a feeling that they were into something shady, deal wise, back then, and they got real close."

She combed Wally's bangs straight and inspected them. "Was there anything that might have caused the relationship to break up?" Wally asked, still worried about Eunice and her scissors.

"Garth." Eunice said that with such disgust that Wally was able to see past her curled lips down her throat. The stale smell of old cigarettes wafted back at her.

"How?"

Eunice dropped her voice even lower. "You can't tell anyone. He went after that brat Roxanna's mother, Ted's wife. If Ted found out, he'd not only call in all his loans, he'd cut Logan into little pieces, since Garth is already dead."

Wally considered that for a minute. "What if Ted did find out and he is the person who killed Garth?"

"I didn't see him around that day," said Eunice.

That didn't necessarily matter, Wally reflected, since the killer could have remained unseen. Even though every one in town knew Ted Donner, it was possible. But just to round out her information, Wally asked, "Did Logan know?"

"Yes, he knew about the wife, and he found out about Roxanna."

"Garth was . . . ?"

Eunice nodded. "That was why Logan started doing Roxanna's morning blowout, even though he hates getting up early."

"When was that?"

"About a week before Garth was killed."

Wally was working that out, while still worrying about her hair. She winced.

Eunice jumped back. "I didn't cut you, did I? I have never . . ."

"No," Wally interrupted. "I'm just worried that my bangs will be too short."

Eunice laughed. "You're just like a former client of mine. She was always worried about that. And I was always trying to convince her to wear her hair away from her face, considering her age and all."

Something on Wally's face must have asked a question, because Eunice put her hand on Wally's arm and shook her head.

"I don't mean your age. She was older. And also, this was a few years ago, soon after Garth came to work here." Eunice looked speculative. "I've always wondered if it was my suggestion or his bragging about screwing some guy over when he was younger that made her stop coming to get her hair done. I guess I'll never know about that one."

Wally's ears perked up. "Garth said something about someone that made your client upset? Did she know him?"

Eunice scowled. "I don't know."

Realizing that this was probably nothing, Wally still pursued it. "Who was she?"

"Uh, well, I'm not sure." Eunice shook her head. "And it could have just as easily been about the bangs."

"All the same," said Wally, "could you figure out who it was? Do you still have her file card?"

"I probably do. And if I do, it'll be easy to be sure it's the right card, because it'll say BANGS in red capital letters. I still remember writing that." She laughed. "I'll check, and if I find it, I'll tell Crystal. Okay?" She turned Wally toward the mirror. "How's this?"

Wally was afraid to look and peeked each eye open separately. But it looked as if she hadn't had a trim at all and she realized there was only a tiny dusting of hair on the cape.

It cost her twenty-five dollars anyway.

Doubts filled Wally as she drove home. Would Eunice be able to find out who left her styling chair after being offended by something that Garth said? Was there any significance to the incident? Despite the detailed application that Wally knew every new client had to fill out before a stylist at the salon could work on her, the records might not be as complete as Eunice believed. What if she couldn't find the woman, or she'd moved? Wally's stomach was in a total knot by the time she pulled into her driveway. The wedding was only two weeks away.

So it was with some surprise that Wally found a message from Eunice on her machine when she got home. After letting Sammy out to play in the yard, she reached for the phone. Eunice came on the line almost immediately, in spite of Crystal's warnings that it would be unlikely. The older woman's raspy voice sounded out of breath.

"I've only got a second," she warned, "while my client has her hair washed. The woman I was talking about is Georgina Rider. I don't know if that is important, but she certainly was upset with Garth."

Wally was becoming convinced that this was a good lead. "What makes you say that?"

"The more I think about it, the less I think it had to do with her hair."

Gripping the receiver tighter, Wally said, "Oh? How can you be sure?"

"I'll be right there," Eunice called, Wally supposed to her client. Then her voice was closer to the telephone. "We had already finished with her hair when it happened. I remember that she was looking at the back, holding the small mirror, when Garth started talking. She had already seen her bangs."

"What was he saying?" Wally prompted.

"I remember her face," said Eunice, as if she hadn't heard Wally's question. "She was turned toward me, and as Garth talked, her face got real pale, and she became rigid. I had to wait for a second before she got out of the chair. I thought she was having a stroke."

"Eunice," Wally said, trying to get Eunice to stop remembering what things looked like and tell her what she heard. "What did he say?"

"He was talking about an old high school buddy of his, except he didn't sound friendly. He said something about anonymously calling the sport authorities, and reporting his friend as a, um, ah, ringer. Yes, a ringer. I don't know what he meant though."

Something about Georgina Rider's name made Wally think of an article she'd read in the newspaper a while back. Maybe there was a connection. All she had to do was find it.

She thanked Eunice, both for the information, and for how carefully she had trimmed her bangs. If the woman worked anyplace but at the salon, she'd probably consider using her, if anything ever happened to her usual hairdresser.

In her experience, Wally thought that most people were more than a bit reluctant to change hairdressers when they were satisfied. Yet Georgina Rider had stopped going to Eunice rather than return to the place that Garth worked. Maybe she had even been letting her hair grow wild all this time. Maybe she would return now that Garth was dead.

Wally was itching to find out. But first she'd see if she was the one in the newspaper. She tried to use the computer and find it through Google, but her search came up empty.

She called Sammy back in and apologized for the shortness of his time outside, then headed for the library. It took some time to thumb through the old papers, but finally Wally found what she was looking for. It was an obituary for someone named Rudy Rider.

Services for Rudolph L. Rider, 39, of Billings, Montana, will be held at four p.m. tomorrow in Quincy Suburban Funeral Home, Livingston.

Mr. Rider died Saturday in his home.

He was a member of the Livingston High School swimming team for four years, and winner of the state championships in the four hundred and eight hundred meter categories. He later attended Kean College.

Mr. Rider worked as a water safety instructor-lifeguard at the Summit YMCA for several summers. He also worked as a counselor-swim instructor at Camp Nejeda, a camp for children with diabetes. He was a peer counselor and won the Star Ledger award given to prominent high school volunteers in his junior year.

Born in Livingston, he lived in many states before moving to Montana earlier this year.

Surviving are his mother, Georgina Rider, and a sister, Katinka.

Wally stared at the obituary, wondering how this was possibly related to Garth Barkley. She asked the librarian how to check his obit, and scurried back to her carrel with the photocopy.

The only correlations that she could see were that Garth appeared to have died on the afternoon of Rudy's funeral. They both went to Livingston High School and were on the swimming team. Garth was two years younger than Rudy, presumably they could have known each other, although the years of Rudy's swimming accomplishments were undetermined. Garth's obituary was much longer, listing many more activities, although not one of them was of an altruistic nature.

She also noticed that no mention of a degree for Rudy was made, nor a profession. He seemed to have been tumbleweed since he lived in New Jersey, like a man unable to find a place for himself. In contrast, Garth had a place which many people would have thought adequate, but he was so filled with malevolence that he constantly hurt those around him. She had the sense that their paths had crossed, and possibly that event had impacted at least one of them.

In any case, the deaths of the two men were tragic. Wally had tears in her eyes as she returned the originals of the obituaries. All she could do was mumble thanks before she rushed out of the library.

Chapter Nineteen

The gray-haired woman who answered the door did not have bangs, but her hair was well styled. Wally thought that Eunice would be pleased.

"Mrs. Rider? I'm Wally Morris. I called a little while ago."

"Yes," said the woman, "please come in."

The room that Mrs. Rider led Wally into was attractively furnished. Everything was tidy, dusted, and neat, but the room seemed sad. The only bright spots were the pictures, many of a teen age boy with rippling muscles and a skimpy bathing suit, poised on a swimmer's starting block waiting for a race, or posing on a platform with a medal. There were framed medals and several trophies standing on the mantel. Wally assumed they were Rudy's, the young man who died just before Garth.

"You said on the phone that you were wondering about something I might have heard, and that it was important."

Wally nodded, and explained why she needed the information. "I think it may be the link we need to help the police find the murderer. The only problem is, the victim is someone you may not want to hear about."

"I know who you mean," said Mrs. Rider. "And I don't like to think about him. But if I can help you, it is my duty."

"Can you tell me what he said that upset you?"

"He was bragging about something he did to my son."

Wally was stunned. She knew it was something that made the woman leave the salon and never return, but this was closer to the bone than she'd expected. "May I ask what?"

"He called the New Jersey State Interscholastic Athletic Association and told them that my son was ineligible to swim competitively because he was too old."

"Was that true?"

"Yes and no. We had never tried to hide the fact that Rudy was older than usual for his grade. He got a late start."

She didn't elaborate. Later starting of kindergarten and retention had been accepted practices for years, but they did not usually preclude someone from competing in sports. This seemed to have been caused by some other reason.

Mrs. Rider must have seen the question that lingered on Wally's face, because she answered it. "It wasn't something he could be excluded for, as the investigation showed, but while it was being looked into he missed some key races, and actually ended up losing a wonderful scholarship." She shook her head. "He was so bright, he really shouldn't have lost that scholarship. But the schools thought he was retained for being slow, and I think they were also afraid he'd lose his eligibility."

"Was that possible?"

"I don't know. The guidance counselor didn't know either. And in the end, it didn't matter. He didn't make it in college."

That had been obvious to Wally when she read the obituary. "Do you think that it was because of Garth?"

"I do. And in many ways, I think Garth got what was coming to him. Too bad Rudy never knew that Garth was killed. I hate to say it, but I think he would have been glad."

"I'm so sorry about your son," said Wally.

A tear, which had been building in Mrs. Rider's left eye, spilled over onto her cheek. Another in her right eye poised on the brink. "Thank you. It has been difficult. I wouldn't have been able to get through it without Katinka."

Wally thought about what a lovely name that was. The family name was not particularly Eastern European, but the first names of the mother and children were, and matched this woman's face. Even though she knew from the obituary, she asked, "Is Katinka your daughter?"

"Yes. She adored Rudy. It hurt her so much when all of that happened in high school. I worried for her as much as for him."

Mrs. Rider sighed, and explained that her daughter dropped out of high school right after Rudy's failure in his first year of college and ran off with a totally unsuitable fellow. "The marriage lasted less than six months, and she was back. Somehow I convinced her to get a GED."

"She was with you during the time of Rudy's funeral?"

Georgina wiped her eyes again. "We talked late into the evening the night before the funeral. We remembered the good times, and I confided what I'd heard of the betrayal by Garth. I told her that he was still bragging about it, and I couldn't stop crying. She made me a cup of tea, and sat with me until I fell asleep. I slept better than I had since we got that terrible phone call from Montana. When I woke up it was three in the afternoon. My sister had cleaned the whole house and was impatiently tapping her foot and telling me it was almost time to go to the funeral. Katinka was down in the kitchen, dressed in black, and I knew I had to face the day."

"It was good that Katinka could be with you," said Wally.

Georgina nodded. "She took care of everything. Right after the funeral she went to Montana and gathered Rudy's things. I couldn't have done it."

"That must have been hard for her."

"I think it was. I could see how upset she was, tightly gripping her carry-on bag and her suitcase as she left for the airport. But when she came back, she seemed much calmer, even though she didn't have the carry-on bag. I guess she lost it, but she didn't seem to mind." Georgina stood up. "Do you have any more questions?"

Wally did, but none that she needed to bother Georgina with. She knew Mrs. Rider had an alibi; Rudy's funeral was the afternoon of the day of the murder, and she was sleeping until right before then. Besides, it was surely impossible for this woman to have killed Garth. She'd have been knocked over in the struggle. But the daughter intrigued her, as did the lost carry-on bag.

"It was very good of you to see me," said Wally, as she walked to the door. "My condolences again."

She felt Georgina Rider's eyes on her as she got into her car. It must be so painful. Wally wondered if there was more pain to come. Somehow, she had to find out if it was possible that Katinka Rider had attempted to avenge her brother. And if so, how.

Elliot cracked his knuckles for the third time. He was jumpier than usual, getting nowhere on the case.

Making an effort to stop, Elliot shifted in his seat. But within seconds, he found himself drumming his fingers, going over questions in his mind. He pulled the yellow legal pad he'd been doodling on closer and looked to see if there was anything useful on it.

The only thing written was that Logan Fletcher was hiding information about Garth from his silent partner. Elliot had still never found any investment of Garth's that would explain his partnership in the salon. An indented subheading read, (A) Did Fletcher kill Barkley because Barkley had something on him, something big enough to give him a piece of the salon without a financial investment? Or (B) Did the silent partner, Ted Donner, who also owned the burned-out photography studio property, kill Garth for his interest in both his wife and daughter?

So far they seemed to be the best possible suspects, but Logan was seen by several people, or so they claimed, and the partner was in his office, verified by his secretary. She was very young, Elliot remembered, and the possibility existed that she might have a relationship with her boss that would make her lie for him. It wouldn't be out of character for Donner to have such a connection, according to the data. Then there were all the less likely suspects. He decided to check with Dominique, to see what progress she had made in eliminating them.

But the news from the local police force was negative.

"I'll let you know if I hear anything else," Dominique promised. "Sorry I couldn't help you more now."

After hanging up, discouraged, Elliot wondered if another visit to the area might not help his investigation. It was the only thing he could think to do. Grabbing his jacket, he left his tiny office.

After leaving a message on Elliot's machine to look into someone named Katinka Rider, Wally went to Louise's house to make sure that everything was ready for her imminent return. It was a friendly service each provided for the other during vacations when no one else was home. Michelle, the Fisch's daughter, was still in England doing some of her college work there, and their son, David, was in med school, working around the clock, according to his mother.

Wally brought a quart of milk and a loaf of bread, as well as some fruit and cereal and a frozen casserole that she had in her freezer. Letting herself in the back door with her key, she went to put the groceries away in Louise's soft yellow kitchen. It was the first time that Wally had been there since Louise and Norman went on vacation because a neighbor was watering the plants and the mail was being held at the post office.

But she found a pile of mail on the counter, dishes in the sink, and several windows open. She had either gotten the date of return wrong, meaning that her friends were already home, or something else was going on.

She discounted the possibility of a squatter, but prickles nevertheless shot up her spine. Shivering them away, she looked for more clues.

Most of the mail on the counter was unopened, but one envelope, sitting by itself, addressed to Louise's son and forwarded here, had been slit open.

It had been years since Wally saw David. He'd been away so long, at college and medical school. Before that he had spent his high school years working as much as possible as a volunteer in the hospital in Livingston. She had barely seen him, she realized, since shortly after his Bar Mitzvah, even though she was so close to Louise.

It was a mystery. Why would someone have opened David's mail? Maybe it was something he was expecting and he'd called and asked whoever was watching the house to open it. She decided to see if she could figure out which neighbor that might be.

Pushing open the door to the hallway, Wally headed for the desk that Louise kept her important papers on. But before she got halfway there she came face to face with David.

Astonished, she had only a few seconds to assess the changes in him since he was a teenager. He had grown even taller than his father, and broadened considerably around the shoulders. His hair, always light, was short and respectable. He looked handsome, this former boy who was practically a doctor.

"Wally," he said, his voice deep. "I should have known you were the intruder."

"Intruder?"

"The neighbor was here two hours ago to water the plants. So I knew it wasn't her. It had to be you, since no one else has keys."

"If I may ask, Sherlock, what are you doing here?"

David raised his eyebrows and a smirk played about his lips. "I thought you were the detective, not me."

Wally chuckled. "Well?"

"I am finished with med school," said David. "As of last month. The only thing I have left is graduation, but that isn't for another week, after my parents come home. So I came back here for a while to get ready to go to my residency since my other plans were canceled. I'm surprised you didn't know."

"Oh," Wally said, "I knew you were nearly done. Louise told me."

"I figured the whole world would know that I am almost an official doctor. My mom is pretty proud." The look on David's face said he was proud of himself as well.

"As she should be," Wally said, heading back to the kitchen to unpack the groceries. "Have you heard from your folks?"

"Yes, Mom called two days ago. They're having a fabulous

time. And she told me to make sure I eat right." He rolled his eyes as he added that last piece.

Wally opened the door of the refrigerator. It was packed with several weeks worth of take out cartons and soda and beer cans. Nothing nutritious. She pushed them aside to put juice and milk on the top shelf.

David, standing right behind her, reached for the O.J. and opened it. After a quick glance at Wally he opened a cupboard and took out a glass.

Wally finished emptying the bags and folded them up. "I'm glad they're having fun, but I sure miss them. Things have been so strange around here. So many problems." She turned to David. "Did you tell them about, you know . . . Oh! Do you even know about it?"

"That murder? Yes, but I didn't tell my parents. They'll find out soon enough."

David put an english muffin from the package Wally bought into the toaster, took out the cream cheese that she'd just put into the refrigerator, and opened some jelly. He seemed to be a very hungry young man. And now he had a better chance of eating right.

"Feel free to eat the casserole," Wally said, making a mental note to bring another.

David's eyes lit up. "Did you make it?"

"Yes."

He was smiling as she left.

Wally walked past the salon on her way to the bank. She waved at Crystal who was pouring coffee for a customer whose back faced Wally in the window. Crystal crooked her finger, and, after checking her watch to see that she still had time, Wally opened the door to the salon. Several people must have been having perms, because even though there was exceptional ventilation in the building, it reeked.

"I suppose you don't even notice the smell," said Wally.

Crystal shrugged. "You, like, get used to it."

Several people in various stages of beautification walked

past the desk. Crystal did not give any indication that she noticed the woman with black paste surrounding her face, or the one with foil packets all over her head, or the one waving her nails in the air, presumably to dry them.

"I guess you have a lot of distractions," said Wally, unable to tear her eyes off a nearly bald woman carrying a wig, and fervently hoping that the woman didn't notice. "So much that you might not notice a murd—?"

Crystal bit her lip.

"I'm sorry," said Wally. "I didn't mean to imply . . ."

The outer door opened and the smell of bagels wafted in, along with a man carrying a large bag of them. As he bent over to put them on the table, one of the cards in his pocket fell out, onto the lap of a woman waiting for one of the operators. She looked at it, and tossed in into the trash can under the table. When she looked back to the book sitting in her lap she appeared startled to see the rear of the bagel man so near her face.

Wally giggled softly. But then something occurred to her, and she went over to the trash can and reached in, pulling out the card that the woman had tossed.

It was for a discount at the bagel store, $7.00 for a lox platter, a pretty good deal, considering how high they piled the lox. She looked over at Crystal, with a question forming on her lips.

"Are you, like, asking me to lunch?" the receptionist asked, giggling.

"Not exactly, although that would be fun. But I wondered. Do you remember that one of the witnesses said she saw a solicitor?"

"We don't allow solicitors in here."

"But what if this was what she meant?"

Crystal scowled. Suddenly her eyes widened. "You'd better ask her."

For a moment, Wally thought that over. Gertie was obviously confused, and the possibility that the flyer from the bagel place proved that she knew what she was talking about was slim. After all, she had sworn she saw Doctor Fisch, and he wasn't even a doctor.

Thunderstruck, Wally realized that she might have meant David Fisch. Maybe this woman knew that the pharmacist's son was in medical school and had seen him somewhere since he got home. In a snap decision, Wally decided that the bank could wait. She drove over to Tillie's building and went to see Gertie.

Wally felt rather sheepish as she knocked on the door.

"I hope you remember me," she began, when the woman opened the door.

The look she got in response said that not only did Gertie remember her, she also remembered their last conversation, in which Wally implied that Gertie's memory was not good at all. "I wish you would forgive me . . ." Wally added, not really sure how to finish the sentence.

Gertie motioned for Wally to come into the apartment. "I certainly remember you. As to forgiving you, I'd have to know why."

She seemed much less nervous than usual. Wally wondered what had happened.

"I, that is, er . . ."

"When I had students in my class I was always as patient as I could be with them," said Gertie. "But they were usually more prepared than you."

With sudden clarity, Wally realized who Gertie was. Norman Fisch had once mentioned something about her having taught in the high school when he attended, all those years ago. It was just possible that Gertie had been his teacher, and had kept special track of him, including knowing that his son was planning to become a doctor. Which gave even more credence to her observation.

"You meant that you saw David when you said that you saw Dr. Fisch, didn't you."

"Yes."

"Why didn't you say that?"

"I did. If I remember correctly, you told me that the pharmacist was out of town. That did not exactly address the issue, did it?"

Wally felt like a ninth grader herself. "No, I guess it didn't."

Gertie had a self satisfied look on her face, but that disappeared, replaced by a questioning gaze.

Wally cleared her throat. "I wanted to ask you about the solicitor. The salon says that they do not allow solicitors, but you said you saw one."

"I did. And by the look on your face, you now believe me."

"It was a bagel flyer, wasn't it? Why didn't you tell the police that you were sure?"

Gertie's upright posture seemed to disintegrate in front of Wally. "Because I did think, at that time, that I was losing my mind. Everything pointed that way. But then you found that money. I suppose I should be more gracious about this."

"I understand. And I am really sorry."

"Thank you." Gertie sat up straight, but seemed to be fighting her emotions. "I was sure I saw all those people, at least sometime that day." She looked Wally in the eye. "Will you tell the police?"

Wally nodded, forcing a smile. "Yes."

Chapter Twenty

A persistent feeling that the key to the mystery was Rudy Rider's sister haunted Wally at the same time that it made her a bit giddy. She wished Elliot would call back with some information. In the meantime, while she was unwilling to ask poor Mrs. Rider anything else herself, she realized that other people might know something about Katinka. Maybe someone could give her some background, some clue to how her mind worked.

She dialed Tess Barkley, Garth's last wife, who incidentally owed her a favor for getting information about her fiancé, the movie theater owner.

Wally inquired about how Tess's daughter was handling the death of her father and Tess told her about her wedding plans which were on hold until the little girl was ready for another major change in her life. Then Wally explained why she had called.

"I met him way after high school," said Tess. "Maybe you should call Sally. I think she went to high school with him."

So Wally got that phone number and dialed. Sally said that no, she didn't go to high school with Garth, Rita did. But she kept Wally on the line anyway, telling her how much she had loved Garth, and that now that he was gone forever, she was only hanging in for their little girl. Without being rude, Wally got her off the phone as quickly as possible. And after all that talking, Wally didn't find out anything, because Rita wasn't home and Wally could only leave a message.

Elliot was only home for a minute before he dialed his office to pick up any messages that might have come in since he left. He had expected to hear from the fire department about the cause of the photography studio fire, but there were no messages from the arson investigators or anyone else.

Since it had been a hot, sticky day, he took a shower before dinner. Unfortunately, there was no way to wash off his encounter with Ted Donner, during which he questioned him about what he knew of Garth's relationships with his family. The man was the type who thought that his time was worth way more than anyone else's, and he tried to dismiss Elliot by pointing out that he not only had a strong alibi, he also had no motive. But Elliot refused to be rushed out, and sat down in one of the chairs facing Donner. The office had the plushest carpet Elliot had ever seen, and the deeply polished mahogany desk took up more space in the room than there was in Elliot's entire cubicle.

Ted Donner stood for MONEY, Elliot knew. He owned enough real estate in three counties that his taxes alone could support a local police department for several months. His suits were Italian, finely cut, so much so that his paunch nearly disappeared. His Italian shoes and blown dry hair seemed to fit with the cologne he wore. Elliot hid a smile, thinking that it might be called 'Eau de Big Bucks.'

The man was self-confident, telling Elliot that he was at a fund raiser with five hundred other people during the time the photo studio burned to the ground. "I don't know how it happened," he said. "I suppose I'll have to listen to some more idiots claiming I had something to do with it, but I'll live with it." He smiled.

But his smile and poised calm faded when Elliot told him about Mrs. Donner's adulterous afternoons with Garth, and Garth's morning gropings with Roxanna.

Donner turned bright red, and nearly reached over his desk

to grab Elliot's throat. "You're insane!" he'd shouted. "Get out of my office."

Elliot felt sweat break out on his forehead. "Sir," he'd said quietly, "I know this is hard to believe. But there were several people who witnessed the liaisons."

"Are you saying that you have someone who saw Garth Barkley with my wife?"

"We have motel registrations and receptionists, yes. And several employees at Resplendence saw Garth try to seduce your daughter. That was why she switched hairdressers."

Donner leaped up and paced around his office. At first the man denied any such possibility, but then he seemed to crumple up. There was no question in Elliot's mind that the real estate mogul knew nothing about it before now.

"I thought I had enough problems with that slime ball when he cheated my niece out of the apartment building I'd signed over to her. Hell, I should have killed him the day he walked into the salon!"

"Excuse me," said Elliot. "Did you say that your niece . . . ?"

Donner sat down. "Lexie. She works at the salon. She's cute, but nothing upstairs, y'know? So I thought she couldn't do any better than Garth-Lowlife-Barkley. She made the mistaken assumption that he was really going to marry her, so she signed over the building to him. I should have killed him when he dumped her. I was all set to file a lawsuit over the building when he was murdered." He flexed his fingers, as if he were crushing someone's windpipe. Elliot got chills.

"Now," Donner continued, "you tell me he was with my wife. *My* wife? And trying to get to my little girl? Was he insane? He's lucky he's a dead man. I wouldn't have let him die so quickly. I would have made it slow torture." He had been walking around again, but he sat down abruptly. "I'm gonna get Logan, for letting all of this happen. And my wife. They are going to pay."

Elliot wouldn't want to be Logan Fletcher when Ted Donner got over his shock and began to seek retribution. He wouldn't want to be his wife or his daughter either. The man was still muttering curses at his family and former friend Logan when Elliot left.

Garth left a lot of trashed lives littered on the road. Yet there didn't seem to be a way to figure out which one had been harmed enough to actually kill the man. So many of Garth's victims were female, and few women were strong enough to have tangled with Garth and won.

Rita returned Wally's call after she came home from her last aerobics class. The two women decided to meet for an iced tea. Wally wanted to talk about Rudy Rider in person and figured she had a better chance of getting the whole story if she were face to face with Garth's first wife.

They met in town in one of the newly opened coffee chains. Rita, wearing spandex shorts and a tank top, seemed to be cold in the highly air-conditioned shop, because she ordered a hot latte instead of a cool drink. Wally had the same thing, though iced. While Rita added sweetener to her drink, Wally studied her diamond engagement ring. Rita told Wally how she'd been afraid for so long to commit to another marriage, after Garth. They chatted about weddings before Wally steered the conversation to business.

"Sure I remember," Rita said, when Wally asked her about Rudy. "We were both on the high school swim team, although he was a few years ahead of me. Rudy was a really sweet guy. Garth made mincemeat out of him, calling him all kinds of names in public." She frowned, remembering. "Rudy seemed to let it roll off his back, but was notified by the school that his credentials were under review by the athletic association. He had to stay out of several competitions." She shook her head sadly. "He never got over it."

"Why did the athletic association review his eligibility?" asked Wally.

Rita furrowed her brows. "I didn't get the details, but as I understand it, Rudy was older than he should have been as a senior. He was already twenty. So the association wanted to make sure he was still a bona fide student in the high school."

That was basically what Mrs. Rider had said. But it didn't explain much, nor did it show what Rudy's classmates might have thought at the time. "Do you know why was he that old?" Wally asked.

"He had some kind of problem when he was younger," she said. "He once told me about it, although I don't remember the exact details. Apparently, for some reason he was deaf, which I guess he got over, and so he didn't start school until he was almost eight."

"Why wasn't he in a special school?" Wally asked.

Rita shrugged. "I'm not sure. I remember him saying once that he couldn't go to a special school because the doctors couldn't find anything wrong, but since he could never hear and he couldn't speak very clearly, he couldn't go to a regular one." She paused. "I know it doesn't make a lot of sense. But then one day he was able to hear, he said. Or maybe he had an operation, because he got over the deafness, but he was really far behind. He did the early grades quickly, skipping several, but then he slowed down to one year at a time. I used to feel bad about it, but he had a pretty good attitude until that thing came up with the swimming. In the end he was cleared to swim, but the season was over. He was never the same afterward. I don't even think he showed up for graduation. I know he didn't go to the prom. I was invited by another senior and I had been kind of hoping he'd ask me to dance, but . . ."

She broke off, leaving silence. Wally had so much to think about, she barely knew where to start. "Garth was the one who told the swimming people, wasn't he?"

Rita gasped. "You're kidding, aren't you? Even Garth couldn't be that mean."

"Would he have had anything to gain from doing that?" asked Wally.

"I guess he might," said Rita. "It put Garth into the top spot on the team. Rudy lost the position of captain during that time." She paused. "Do you think Garth did that?"

"I have some reason to believe it," said Wally. "And if that is the case, do you think it may have had something to do with Garth's death?"

Rita shook her head. "If I remember correctly, Rudy was dead before that. He couldn't have done it."

"So you know about that." Wally wondered what else Rita knew. "Do you know if it was suicide?"

Rita sniffled. "That's what I heard." She reached for a tissue, choking Wally up too.

Wally tried not to let her voice quaver. "I thought so."

"How does this help you?" asked Rita.

Wally answered that with a question. "Do you know anything about Rudy's family?"

"I used to see his mother around, and sometimes his little sister. She was so cute, the way she looked up to him. She came to all the meets. But I haven't seen either one of them in years." She dropped her voice and said with remorse, "I wasn't able to go to the funeral."

Wally wanted to ask more about the sister. Like, was she really big for a woman? Or did she have a relationship with a man who might have wanted to make Garth pay for her brother's suicide? But how to phrase it? "His sister . . ."

"Rudy used to call her Tink," said Rita, "but she hated that almost as much as her real name, which she thought was too old fashioned."

Wally could sympathize with that.

"I wonder how she is," Rita continued. "It must have been so hard for her when Rudy . . ." She broke off, leaving the obvious unsaid.

Wally continued to probe. "You haven't heard anything?"

"I know she still lives around here somewhere. She . . . I think I heard she got married, but it didn't last."

That was what Wally had heard from Mrs. Rider. It didn't add anything useful to what she already knew. "Is there any more?" she asked, hopefully.

Rita sighed loudly. "I wish there was something I could do to help. If only someone could tell us who killed Garth, then we could all get on with our lives."

Wally hadn't realized that Rita had been so impacted by

her ex-husband's death. There were no children between them, after all. But it became more clear when Rita added, shivering, "It's like a shadow. I want to get out from under this cloud and into the sun."

When Wally said goodbye to Rita, she felt the same way.

Chapter Twenty-one

"I'll be waiting."

Wally hung up the phone with joyful anticipation. She couldn't wait to see Louise, her long lost hula-loving friend. Rushing to the freezer, she pulled out a coffee cake to thaw. Then she put on a fresh pot of coffee and set the table. By the time she was ready, Louise, wearing a Hawaiian flowered sundress, floated through the door.

"Yes, I love you too," she said to Sammy, pushing the black Labrador retriever off herself and down to the floor.

Wally gazed at her friend's glowing skin. With a complexion that went with her red hair and heavy anti-aging sun block use, she didn't really tan, but after a month in the sun of Hawaii, Louise looked golden and terrific. Every inch of her long-limbed frame seemed to radiate relaxation and health. Wally was envious. "Wow."

"I highly recommend the trip. You and Nate should go right after the wedding. Which reminds me, what's wrong?"

After pouring the coffee and taking the cake out of the microwave, Wally put it on the table and sat down. She told her friend about the murder, which drew quite a barrage of questions and comments from Louise, as did the investigation.

"I can't believe I missed all of this," Louise said. "But on second thought, it's okay." She held out her hands as if they were imaginary scales. "Hawaiian paradise," she said, moving her right hand down. "Murder and mayhem," she continued, moving her left hand very little. "I think we can guess which one would win."

"I thought you'd think that." Wally vented a bit of the anxiety she felt at not having her friend around. "And you left me with all this mess."

"Admit you love it."

"Sure, I love seeing dead bodies and hearing about everyone's dirty little secrets. I live for it."

Louise frowned. "Cut the sarcasm. Your only problem is that there are too many suspects and not enough clues."

"You're right," Wally agreed, "I'm frustrated. Tell me about your trip."

"It was fabulous. The entire trip, well not the entire trip." She giggled. "Actually, I never thought we were going to get there."

"Why?"

Louise leaned back as much as she could in the ladder back kitchen chair. Her hair was practically orange today, probably from the sun, although Wally suspected it would be back to normal soon, once Louise went to the hairdresser to get her half-inch roots colored.

With her warm, brown eyes dancing in merriment, Louise launched into her story. "The plane for California, since we had to do a stop over because we booked too late to get a non-stop flight to Hawaii thanks to Norman's indecision, took off from Newark airport at least an hour late. The pilot came on the loudspeaker and welcomed us, like they always do, and they showed the movie about what to do in a crash and what a great airline we had chosen. Then there was a gigantic clunk, with no explanation, and the flight attendants were just setting things up like nothing had happened. I wouldn't have worried, but the plane wasn't getting any higher; when we leveled out we could still see the people in the cars on the turnpike. I actually turned to Norman and asked him how high we were, and how high the Rockies were and how were we going to get over them."

"What was going on?"

"We didn't know, and everyone started asking. The man in front of Norman asked the flight attendant what the loud clunk was and she said, 'What clunk?' Except something was happening, because there was black stuff streaming out of the wings."

Louise sipped her coffee. Wally waited, and when her friend put down her cup, she urged her to continue.

"Norman explained that they were dumping fuel which made me wonder even more how we would get to California. Finally the pilot got on and announced that we would be returning to the airport. He said there was nothing to worry about. But when we landed back at Newark, it was in a far away section of the airport, near where the UPS planes are and we were instantly surrounded by emergency vehicles and fire trucks that spray that foam stuff on the runway."

Louise paused, but something she had said had Wally's mind wandering. It took her away from the present into a dark fuzzy corridor where something nagged at her.

Her friend was looking at her expectantly, she realized, when Louise said, "Are you listening?"

"Of course," Wally replied. "Did you have to go down a chute?"

"No. They must have decided that we weren't going to catch on fire, because they taxied over to the gate and we got off onto a bus which took us back to the terminal." She took another sip of coffee.

"So what was wrong?"

"You could see it plainly through the bus window. The fan thing inside one of the engines was broken. We had hit a goose."

"And . . ."

"So when we get back inside the airport all of these Hollywood types started running around making calls on their cell phones."

"How did you know they were Hollywood types?"

"Oh, you know. They were half balding men with ponytails. And their clothes! Practically like a uniform of strangeness. So there they all were, calling people and changing meetings and the rest of us were waiting to find out what gate to go to for the new plane."

Wally could picture it clearly. But what she'd said started up that niggling feeling she got when she was supposed to remember something important. If only she could pinpoint it.

"But there wasn't any plane," Louise continued. "That had been the last one for the night. We had to wait until the next morning. And Norman thought it was an omen, that we shouldn't go because something would go wrong." She stopped speaking.

The lack of chatter roused Wally. "Obviously you went. And had a great time. Thanks for telling me." She stood up and started clearing the table.

"I haven't told you anything yet. As far as you know we were still at the airport. My ears weren't even clogged yet."

Wally gasped.

Louise cocked her head at Wally. "What's up?"

Wondering where all the air in the room had suddenly gone, Wally said, "Up?"

"I can see that you have that look on your face."

Wally felt dizzy, as if all the blood had drained out of her head. It couldn't be. There had to be another explanation.

But what it was evaded her. She was just left with the obvious.

Louise trailed right behind Wally as she ran to the phone. "Who are you calling?"

"Elliot." Quickly hanging up, Wally turned to her friend. "No. I have to be sure." She ran outside.

"Where are you going?" Louise called after her.

Wally came back into the house. "Nowhere. Your car is behind mine. I never thought I'd say this to you, but could you please leave?"

"Forget it. I'll drive you wherever you want to go, as long as you tell me what's going on. Maybe I can help."

Wally thought about that. Of all the people in the world, Louise was the only one she wouldn't mind being wrong in front of. And she really wanted to be wrong. "Okay."

As soon as Louise's Cadillac was out of the driveway and

on the street and Wally had pointed out which direction they should go, she went over what Louise said. "Tell me again," she asked her friend, "about where the plane landed."

"Why? It wasn't much. We landed, the trucks came . . ."

"No. Where you landed. A remote section of the airport."

"Oh," said Louise. She followed Wally's hand signal to turn right at the corner. "By the freight planes. Fedex, DHL, UPS."

"That's it."

"What?"

Without answering, Wally pressed her questions. "And what did you say about the Hollywood types?"

"About their cell-phones?"

"No, what they were wearing."

"It wasn't anything special. Just typical stereotype stuff, which is why I thought it was so funny."

"You called them a uniform."

"But it wasn't."

Wally stared at the road. "But it reminded me. That and the thing about your ears. Turn here."

Louise turned an open-mouthed face at Wally, but seemed to reconsider and look back at the road. "Where are we going?"

"To Tillie's building."

"We're going to see your mother-in-law?"

"Not exactly. A neighbor of hers. And come to think of it, I'm glad you're here."

"I'm sure you'll tell me why," said Louise. They parked, and walked toward the building entrance.

"Well, part of the mystery involves your husband, and your son."

Louise shook her head. "I'm suffering from jet-lag, could you please explain yourself?"

As quickly as she could, Wally explained the mixed-up sightings of the male Fisches. "When I called David about it," Wally said, "he told me he had accidentally walked into the salon for a minute, because he wasn't paying attention. He went right out again, and into the Chinese restaurant next door."

"King of take-out," said Louise. "And in that second Norman's old teacher Gertie saw him?"

Wally nodded. "I guess."

They walked down the hall to Gertie's apartment. Wally knocked. "I just want to be sure." As much as she wanted to prove herself wrong, she thought. If only.

They heard shuffling and after a while, the door opened. Gertie blinked at them a few times.

Wally reminded her of who she was and introduced Louise, who assured Wally she and Gertie were old friends. Wally turned and stared at Louise.

Gertie invited them inside. "What can I do for you?"

"I'm still embarrassed about not believing you," Wally started. "And so sorry." She waited for Gertie to acknowledge her apology, then continued, reluctantly. "I have to ask about one more person you said you saw."

"Who?"

"Well, when I was here, you said, after the solicitor thing was straightened out with the coupon from the bagel place, and the mistake with Mr. Fisch and Dr. Fisch was cleared up . . ."

Gertie smiled at Louise. "I almost forgot. Congratulations."

"Thank you." Louise smiled back, puffed up with pride.

Wally cleared her throat. "The other thing you said was that you saw the UPS person."

"That's true."

"But Crystal and the police say that isn't possible that you saw a UPS man."

Gertie looked at her, narrowing one eye. "I didn't say it was a man. Didn't you ever hear of a female UPS person?"

A shiver ran down Wally's spine. "Yes," she said. "One delivers to my house. Could you excuse me for a minute?"

Not even waiting for a response, Wally took out her cell phone and dialed her next door neighbor's number, barely breathing while she waited for her to answer. She could only hope that Marla wasn't out driving one of her millions of car pools.

"Marla," said Wally, as soon as the woman answered the

phone. "Do you remember when you were telling me about a woman who told you to check Tabitha for a hearing problem?"

"Yes."

"You said she was a stranger. Do you know who she was?"

"What?" Marla laughed, although it was not a purely happy sound since she was obviously wondering where Wally was going with her sudden questions. "No. She wasn't a total stranger. You probably know her, being married to the great mail-order king."

"You mean Niki?" Wally struggled to keep her voice steady. "She's the one who told you about the milk allergy causing hearing problems? The one whose brother had the same thing?"

Marla nodded. "I was really upset one day just as she came to deliver a package. She asked me why and I told her about Tabitha's deafness."

"You said a stranger," Wally insisted, wishing it wasn't true.

"Sorry. I didn't mean it literally, just that it wasn't a doctor or someone you'd expect to tell you about a cure for deafness. Why do you want to know?"

"I can't explain it, but thanks, Marla. I'll talk to you soon. Oh, and please don't mention this call to anyone."

Niki, thought Wally, hanging up the phone. Could she be Katinka, as in Rider? Niki was a reasonable nickname, better than Tink, and everything else fit. "Are you saying you saw a female UPS driver that afternoon, Gertie?"

"I am. Do you believe me now?"

"I think I should. The odd thing is that the usual delivery was much later in the day."

"I saw what I saw. It isn't like the uniform is hard to pick out, even with limited eyesight."

"Yet no one else saw."

"Well, she didn't stay in the uniform." Gertie paused, cocking her head to one side, almost like a bird. "It must have been a dye job."

"What?"

"Black. She was wearing a black smock the second time I saw her." Gertie shrugged. "What else can I tell you?"

"Tell me what just happened," Louise begged when they were back in her car.

"I'm not sure. How can I get proof?"

"Isn't UPS computerized? Wouldn't that show when the deliveries were made?"

Wally shook her head. "There weren't any that day. And they usually come later."

"But even if there weren't any for the salon, maybe there were others in the neighborhood."

"Oooh, you're so smart, Louise." Wally pored through her bag again for her cell phone and got through to Elliot. But when she was done, she was disappointed all over again. "He said that they checked the records, and the deliveries to the nearby stores were much later in the afternoon. But there must be something to this."

"You've heard the expression, you can't be all wrong, haven't you?"

"Yes. So?"

"Well, maybe Gertie can't be all right."

"We have to follow this up. Drive to the salon."

"Whatever you say, Sherlock."

Crystal seemed pleased to see Wally, and unable to get her eyes off Louise's prominent roots. "What can I do for you?"

"We have reason to believe . . ." Wally stopped, because Louise had put her hand on her arm.

"You have reason." She turned to Crystal. "I have a need for a touch up. Is Armond free?"

Crystal got her squeezed in, and turned back to Wally. "You were saying?"

"Is there any possibility that the UPS carrier was here earlier in the afternoon?"

Crystal thought for a minute. "Only if she, like, had to use the bathroom."

"What do you mean?"

"I didn't see Niki on that day. But she always comes in to use the bathroom."

Wally frowned, with this further confirmation of her theory. She shook off her chills. "So Niki uses your bathroom?"

"Where else is a girl gonna go during the day?"

"I guess I never thought about it."

"Sure," said Crystal. "And she comes a few times a day, just to use the rest room. She goes through the back and straight down to the break room. She doesn't like to go through the salon to the other bathrooms because, as she explained, then everyone would know where she was going and she'd have no privacy."

"I guess that makes sense, sort of."

"Does that help?"

"Not really. It isn't what I wanted to hear." Almost to herself, she mumbled, "She would never do that, though."

Crystal eyes widened. "You can't think that she . . . The police said it was a man."

Wally blinked. "How did you know that?"

Crystal blushed. "Ryan told me."

Wally pretended not to notice the blush and stuck with the odious business at hand. "I suppose a woman who delivers packages for a living might be strong enough." She shivered. "What am I saying? It couldn't have been Niki. She was off that day. Do you remember?"

"Um, I'm not sure. How do you know that?"

"She delivers to my house, too, and there was a delivery that afternoon. It was a different carrier." Simultaneously the realization that the grieving Rider girl would have been off from whatever job she had, hit Wally. Katinka Rider, possibly Niki, had to go to her brother's funeral. Her brother was deaf as a child and got over it, like her neighbor, Marla's, little girl. The UPS person, Niki, told Marla how to cure the deafness. The circle kept going around. Wally closed her eyes. Please don't let it be true.

"Maybe Jamal . . ." Crystal suggested, not finishing her sentence.

"Who?"

"Jamal. He's the carrier who filled in for Niki that week. He told me the day after the funeral that she was off for some family thing."

That didn't help Wally feel any better. The Rider girl would have been off from her job, to go to Montana and bring back her brother's things. It was becoming far too much for coincidence.

Wally knew she was grabbing at straws, but she asked Crystal what she'd meant when she brought up Jamal.

"Maybe he was the UPS person spotted here that day."

"Gertie said it was a woman. She was sure."

Crystal laughed. "Maybe it was a man with a pony tail."

Wally clutched at the straw offered by Crystal. That was probably it. Best two out of three for Gertie, maybe, like Louise said. Except that didn't fit with Jamal. Would there have been two substitutes?

She asked Crystal not to mention anything. Waving to Louise, who had changed into a black smock and was covered in a plastic cape and hair color, she left the salon and walked home. She clung to a tiny hope that she was wrong about Niki, that it was someone else with a similar background. But she had to prove it, one way or the other.

Chapter Twenty-two

Elliot fought the urge to bounce his pencil impatiently while he waited for the supervisor to come to the phone. Instead, he opened the arson investigation file again. There it was, in black and white, the cause of the fire. It wasn't arson, it wasn't even caused by Ted Donner, the owner of the property and one of Elliot's prime suspects. The cause of the fire had been a crock pot that was left on too long in the fortune teller's suite upstairs.

That thought brought back his conversation with the fortune teller. She was the one who told him who owned the property and added to his suspicions about Mr. Donner. He couldn't believe how totally oblivious she was about causing so much trouble for so many people and making her landlord a suspect in a crime.

When Wally called, and Elliot had mentioned that Ted Donner was no longer a suspect, she had told him not to worry about it. But was she right? Was her lead worth looking into? She seemed pretty sure it was, kept saying something about the suicide of someone named Rudy Rider, and sounded angry as anything that he hadn't followed up on a message she'd left about the Riders. He had explained to her that he never got the message. Then she got angry because she couldn't get the information about the UPS deliveries herself.

Although he wasn't sure she had a valid lead, he'd already

talked to the UPS dispatcher, who couldn't answer any questions, and now the supervisor was looking into his questions. He wanted to know whether another driver, someone other than Niki Stetson or Jamal Jenkins, might have been on a route on the afternoon of the murder. Was it possible that they should be looking for someone wearing a brown uniform, either a woman or a man with a pony tail, or was there a reasonable explanation for what Gertie claimed to have seen?

That anyone was giving a moment's thought to what that woman had said seemed ridiculous to Elliot, who clearly remembered how vague she had been when he took the statements of the people in his future grandmother-in-law's building. But Wally seemed convinced that there might be something to it.

After what seemed like another twenty minutes, although it was only two according to Elliot's watch, the supervisor came to the phone. "I can't find any record of delivery to that area in the early afternoon. Our regular carrier was off for the week, and we had a replacement, Jamal Jenkins. But deliveries there are made in the late afternoon."

"Is it possible . . ." Elliot began.

"I wish I could help you," said the man. "I know this is important. I've searched all our records, and also the routes of every driver in that area, but I can't find anyone who was in that town at all that day, besides the sub, later that afternoon. I don't mean to tell you your business, but I think you're barking up the wrong tree. Maybe it was FedEx."

Elliot ignored that suggestion. "Were you able to find out if Niki Stetson uses any other name?"

"Her employment application only says Niki Stetson. Next of kin is Anthony Stetson."

Elliot thanked him and hung up. Not only did he have no connection to the Riders, which Wally thought might have existed, he had no connection to a UPS delivery that day. He was left wondering about the brown uniform. It was possible that someone could have simply been wearing a brown shirt that day and they were entirely on the wrong track. But maybe there was something to what Gertie saw. If she was the only one who saw that person, it was possible that the person was trying not to be seen. If that were true, it was worth looking into.

His phone rang before he could call Dominique and run the whole thing past her.

"This is Abby Kent. You said you wanted to know who introduced me to Garth. I finally remembered."

Elliot had put off calling the young antiques dealer with the good hair style a third time, thinking it was probably immaterial. He took a deep breath. "Who was it?"

"Rudy Rider. At a show at the Armory. And Rudy said Garth wasn't a nice person, but I didn't pay attention."

Gripping the receiver, Elliot said, "Rudy Rider?

Abby told him about the show that all three had attended. Elliot thanked her, feeling he had to look into that Rider connection, which suddenly seemed more plausible, with a much more open mind than he'd shown Wally.

He called Dominique to tell her what he wanted to do. She agreed, after first calling it a long shot, and then he called his future mother-in-law. He filled her in on the connection to the art exhibition, Garth, and the antiques dealer whose picture had been displayed on the sides of buses without her knowledge. Wally gasped when she heard the Rider name.

As she drove to the salon, Wally thought about the call she'd just had from Rita Barkley. A heaviness sat on her heart.

One half hour less than four weeks after the murder, Wally stood in the same position she had while Tillie had her hair permed that day, wondering if they would find the proof they needed. Many of the other people who had come in on that dreadful afternoon were present, some just because they were always there on that day and time of the week, some, like Gertie, at the request of either Wally or Dominique. One obvious difference, as far as Wally was concerned, was that Tillie no longer wore her cast. She had driven over by herself, and Eunice was making a big fuss over her.

"I'll bet you'll dance the night away at your granddaughter's wedding," Eunice said.

Tillie's eyes twinkled. "Those young men will be busy."

Many of the clients who had seen Garth on that day had already found other hairdressers, but two of them who had been there at the time were present, as well as the English woman with the asymmetrical, horrible haircut that had caused her so much distress. Dominique, Ryan, and Elliot were also there.

A few more people were expected, but they would be arriving at the same time they had come in on the day of the murder.

Inspector Davis and his partner were notably absent, having decided that this was a colossal waste of time. But Wally didn't think so, though it might implicate someone she liked and respected. Since there was a little time before the exact moment of the murder, she decided to have a look around.

She wandered over to the back door, going the long way, through the main part of the salon. A new stylist stood at the station that had been Garth's, with a big bouquet of real flowers in contrast to the silk flower arrangements that were all around the salon. Wally had checked with Crystal and knew that she was not one of the people who had been there that morning. In all, three hairdressers who had been there on the morning of the murder were not there today. One was Garth, of course, and the other two had moved on to other jobs, turnover in salons being what it was. "I promise you," Crystal had said, and Dominique had confirmed, "that both were visible during the time of the struggle and murder. We don't need them today."

Wally reached the back door, and went out into the parking lot. Crystal, she knew, was taking inventory of the people entering from the front door, but she wanted to see who came in the back.

A beat-up old car drove up and pulled into the most coveted space outside the salon, the one right next to the handicapped spot. A man of about forty got out and went around to the passenger side of the car. He wore bright green pants with one leg accidentally pushed up and Wally could see that he was wearing short cowboy boots, which seemed out of character with the rest of him.

He had trouble opening the door, and kept putting the key in, trying to unlock it, but only succeeded in relocking the automatic locks. The passenger made no effort to unlock the door from the inside. Instead she, an old lady with improbably pink hair whom Wally recognized as a salon patron of the day of the murder, kept shouting abuses at the man. He finally got her out of the car, but, despite the care he took with her, she was angry at him, and pulled her arm away as soon as she stood up. He handed her a cane, but had to trot after her to go up the steps and hold the door open. She got too close, and had to move back so that the door could swing out, but she seemed impatient to get inside. "One minute, Mother," he pleaded.

As soon as she was inside, he hurried down the steps back to the car, got in, and waited. He didn't read a newspaper, or a book, or even appear to turn on the radio. He just sat there.

It seemed odd that he was available at that time of day, but maybe he always drove his mother to the salon. It made Wally wonder if he could be a suspect, but he seemed way too bumbling for that. She had to wonder, though, if somehow he could have seen something and not been on the list of people to ask.

She knew she should get Elliot or Dominique to come and question the man; that would be the responsible thing to do, so as not to taint any evidence or put any misleading information into his mind. But she was unable to force herself to go back inside. What if he drove away? Or what if he took a nap while he was waiting? That would mean that he might not have been in a position to see anything on the day of the murder.

After five minutes he was still there, still staring in the direction of the back door of the salon. Wally went over to the car, and knocked on the window.

It seemed that in order for him to be able to open the window, he had to turn on the car. The engine roared as he flooded it, and scowling, he fumbled for the window switch.

"Yes?" he said.

Wally explained her questions. It took several minutes, because she wanted to be sure not to influence him in any way, so she didn't come right out and say that she wondered if he saw a female murderer come out of the salon and run away. Instead she just asked him if he was there on the date of the murder at the same time. When he said yes, she asked him to wait and went to find the authorities.

Chapter Twenty-three

Wally took a deep breath to steel herself and opened the door. She ran down the long corridor from the back to the reception area and looked for Dominique.

The din of the salon momentarily distracted her, making her wonder what the murderer saw when she, if it was a she, arrived. The whole place was busy, with hair dryers going and hair being blown, and other hair being washed, or moussed or gelled or colored. Not one person looked in Wally's direction. It would have been so simple to slip into the stairwell, if someone came by, on the way to the consultation room.

Eunice fluffed the front of Tillie's hair. She had picked up a can of spray when Wally spotted Dominique.

Wally pulled her aside and filled the detective in on the man in the parking lot. Dominique's jaw was set as she grabbed Ryan's arm and headed to the back door. Wally stood right where she was, nervously awaiting their return.

Dominique was back in five minutes, with Ryan trailing behind. "He saw her go in," Dom said, beaming. "She came running out a while later, wearing a black smock. He got a good look at her face."

Wally swallowed. "Was it . . . ?"

"Yes. The UPS carrier. I showed him a picture of Niki Stetson that Gertie identified and he ID'd it." Dominique nodded over to Gertie.

Gertie smiled back. "I told you I saw her."

"It explains a lot," said Dominique. "And most incriminating of all, she drove her own car, not a delivery truck."

That had only just begun to sink in to Wally's mind when Dominique continued. "If it was the regular delivery person, you," she pointed at Crystal, "wouldn't necessarily have thought anything was out of place even if you saw her, so she could have had an explanation ready for why she was here when you asked."

Crystal nodded. "Like I said, she came in to use the bathroom." She furrowed her brow. "But I thought it was a man. Ryan said—." She broke off, staring at Ryan, whose face matched his red hair.

The young detective sputtered. "I never . . ."

"Don't worry about it," said Dominique. She turned to Crystal. "Someone who delivers packages for a living would probably be strong enough to take on even a big guy like Garth."

"And her supervisor said she was off that day," said Elliot, "that whole week in fact, because her brother had died. But I'm still unclear on the motive."

"Oh!"

Everyone turned to Wally, who, after her eruption, stared at the floor. She was so sorry for Niki. But she had committed murder. Another life had been ruined by Garth Barkley.

"It all goes back to Rudy Rider," Wally said, "the person who killed himself in Montana." She had all eyes on her as she related her conversation with Rudy and Katinka's mother about Rudy's problems with Garth. She told them about Mrs. Rider telling her daughter on the evening before the funeral what Garth did to Rudy in high school and the bragging that Garth did in the Salon. "She said they talked for a long time and then she drank some tea that her daughter gave her. She didn't awaken until the next afternoon, just before the funeral. It was at four in the afternoon." She paused, letting that time frame register.

"I think Mrs. Rider might have been given a sedative," Wally continued. "When she woke up it was time for the service. She also said that her daughter went out to Montana right after the funeral, and returned minus a carry-on bag."

Elliot shook his head. "But what did it have to do with Niki Stetson?"

"She is Katinka Rider."

"Are you sure?"

"Yes."

"How did you find out?"

"I talked to Rita Barkley again today. She told me that Katinka married a guy named Anthony Stetson. She used the marriage to change her whole name, and I guess she didn't return to it after the marriage dissolved."

"But you thought they were the same person before today," said Elliot. "Why?"

Wally recalled when her next door neighbor, Marla, told her about Niki figuring out what was wrong with her daughter and the milk allergy. She'd said that her brother, and his temporary deafness, kept him out of school. "When I heard about Rudy Rider starting school late, I didn't know it was because he had been deaf. Rita was the one who told me about the deafness, but she thought it was fixed by an operation. It wasn't—his mother had figured out he was allergic to milk, like my next door neighbor's child."

Elliot scowled. "Why didn't you tell me?"

Wally flinched. "I tried to find Katinka Rider on my own, before I connected her to Niki, but I couldn't find out anything. And I did tell you about Rudy."

"I'm sorry," said Elliot. "I could probably have figured this out myself if I had the Rudy Rider connection sooner. We'll need a warrant."

Debbie seemed annoyed with Wally. "How could you have known who the murderer was and not tell Elliot so that he could get this case out of his hair?"

"I haven't known for very long. No, correction, I never knew, I just suspected. How could I have told Elliot?"

"He might have been able to check it out," said Debbie. "As it was, he officially confirmed that Katinka Rider and Niki

Stetson were the same person in five minutes. And it only took two hours for the police in Montana to find the gym bag with the bloody clothes."

Nausea gripped Wally. "How do you know that?"

"Elliot told me. He and I communicate, unlike you and him."

"Isn't that the way it should be?" said Wally. "I'm not marrying him, you are, in six days. And I was only trying to find proof, you know. I wasn't trying to hide anything."

Debbie stared at her. "What am I going to do with you?" She shook her head. "You are incorrigible." She turned to go, then added. "And stubborn. Could you at least try to stay out of trouble until after the wedding? I don't want anything to go wrong."

Wally was somewhat miffed that her daughter didn't think she had everything under control. But all she said was, "I'll try."

Niki Stetson, whose love for her brother and passion for revenge on his tormentor had ruined her life, was arraigned the next morning. There was a picture of her in the newspaper being led into the police station. Normally statuesque Niki looked very small, and defeated. It was terrible to contemplate the outcome.

Wally shuddered to think of poor Mrs. Rider. She had never done anything to deserve her fate.

The newspapers were filled with articles, and all the news stations picked up the story. *Hard Edition* began interviewing people in town about the multiple murders, even going so far as to have the water tested for some kind of paranoia inducing substance. It made no sense to Wally, since the murderer, like the ones in the other cases, had lived outside of Grosvenor.

She dreaded the trial.

There was a tiny moment when the door to the entry to the wedding chapel was opened to allow people to go through that it was possible to see inside. Wally stood, watching her son, Mark, in his spiffy tuxedo with his diamond ear stud winking, help his grandmother down the aisle behind Elliot and his parents. At a signal, the bridesmaids and the other ushers followed. Then the matron of honor, Rachel, looking as beautiful as she had at her own wedding, walked down the aisle, to be met by the best man. Little Jody, carrying a basket of flower petals, went next. Wally, who watched all of that from behind in tiny snippets, felt jealous of the guests who saw the procession from the front. But she knew what they were seeing, it was the same thing she'd seen during the two hours they had spent taking all the wedding photos. And everyone looked stunning. They had decided to wait until after the ceremony to have the cocktail hour, so that there was no chance of spills. Besides, Debbie didn't want to miss a morsel of food after dieting for months to get into her wedding gown.

When the door opened again it was time for Wally and Nate to accompany their breathtaking daughter, whose gorgeous face was hidden behind her veil. A lump the size of Grosvenor settled in Wally's throat, and she held her breath, hoping she wasn't about to ruin her make-up.

They proceeded down the aisle slowly, Wally on Debbie's right and Nate, whose stoic expression belied the tears in his eyes, on her left. Halfway down they stopped, and each reached under the veil for a kiss. Then they left their daughter and walked together, clasping hands tightly with each other, while the bride waited alone for her future husband. He stepped toward her, smiling the biggest smile Wally had ever seen, and taking Debbie's hand, brought her under the Chuppah, with its pink, blue and violet flowers forming a canopy over the couple.

The cantor sang and the rabbi blessed the union. Debbie and Elliot drank from the traditional cup of wine. They exchanged vows and rings, and, at a signal from the rabbi, Elliot stomped on a wrapped glass, signifying the destruction of the temple in Jerusalem. The newlyweds kissed for the first time as husband and wife.

Everyone danced till way past midnight. The wedding was perfect, as Wally always knew it would be.